CAGED HEAT
BLACKMEADOWS PACK 2

NEW YORK TIMES and USA TODAY
BESTSELLING AUTHOR
MILLY TAIDEN

This book is a work of fiction. The names, characters, places, and incidents are fictitious or have been used fictitiously, and are not to be construed as real in any way. Any resemblance to persons, living or dead, actual events, locales, or organizations is entirely coincidental.

Published By

Latin Goddess Press

Winter Springs, FL 32708

http://millytaiden.com

Caged Heat

Copyright © 2019 by Milly Taiden

Edited by: Tina Winograd

Cover: Willsin Rowe

Formatting by Glowing Moon Designs

All Rights Are Reserved. No part of this book may be used or reproduced in any manner whatsoever without written permission, except in the case of brief quotations embodied in critical articles and reviews.

Property of Milly Taiden

January 2019

— For my curvy readers

You can't love anyone else until you love yourself first. Happiness is internal. Make yours, your priority.

Caged Heat

Samira Suarez's grandmother died, bringing her home after five years. Surprisingly, grandma left her millions of dollars and the family got zero. Such a great way to warm her presence into everyone's heart, right? Sam doesn't care about the money except for the line in the will that reads if she dies within thirty days, the family would get the cash. Say what?

Riel Karven, wolf shifter, has been waiting five years for Sam to return. He's been giving her the time she needs to explore the world, but that time is up. He knew she was his mate before she left. Now that she's back, he's keeping her. And he's going to show her what five long years without the woman he wants does to a man. They might need a new bed after this.

When Sam is injured, Riel goes into overprotective mode. Someone in Sam's family wants her dead for the money. He has to hunt down the stalker if he wants to save his mate. Unfortunately, the person they are looking for isn't even on their radar.

PROLOGUE

It stalked her. Sam ran through the Amazon rainforest, sucking air into her deprived lungs. A slimy vine slapped her face as she blindly bulldozed the dense underbrush.

Where was the fucking village?

Even though she tromped and tore through the vegetation, the creature behind her sounded like thunder rolling through the trees.

She should've listened to the tribe's leader. He'd told her the temple was guarded by a giant wolf—with giant-ass teeth—but she chalked it up to superstition and myths.

The healing herbs she needed only grew on that ground. The medicine in the forest had been used up, leaving the temple land her single choice.

Fortunately, she'd gotten a handful of the leaves before the beast discovered her. But now she was paying the price, well, if it caught her.

The trees were starting to thin and the wild brush had vanished. She was close to the camp.

"Help!" She shouted the names of the men she knew. They didn't understand much English, but she thought they'd figure it out by her tone.

Two women with water jugs on their heads turned to her. Screams ripped from their throats as they dropped the ceramic containers and ran.

Midstride, Sam felt the toe of her boot catch a tree root. Crashing to the ground, she yelled again. Just as an arrow zipped above her, she felt a sharp pain on the bottom of her leg.

The arrow hit dead center of the wolf's head, but the damage was done.

The damn animal had bitten her.

ONE

Sam walked into the hotel in a rush. Her trainers squeaked on the pristine marble floor. She'd been delayed for the reading of her late grandmother's will.

The hotel was one of the better ones in the city with its large, open lobby, gleaming walls, and colorful furniture. She winced at her jeans and T-shirt. After traveling for almost twenty-four hours, all she wanted to do was find a bed and crash.

Unfortunately, that was the last thing she'd be able to do since the lawyer was waiting on her before he could get started. Carajo!

A couple moved toward the elevators. It was the daughter of one of her grandmother's old friends. She waved but didn't have time to stop and chat.

At the front desk, she asked for the location of the meeting room. The desk clerk pointed her in the direction of the elevators, where she entered the cab and hit the button for the third floor.

Jonas Carson had made things easy for everyone by arranging the meeting at the hotel where most of the out-of-town family was staying. Hauling her luggage behind her, she headed for the door she'd been instructed to.

Frustrated with the long dark tendrils escaping her plait, she brushed the hair behind her ear and focused on the task at hand. Her gut clenched with waves of anxiety. She wanted to turn the other way, but Grandma Ginny hadn't raised a sissy. With her shoulders squared, she turned the handle and stepped into the conference room.

Conversation stopped as all eyes turned to glare at her. She lifted a haughty brow in response. A tall, lanky, older man in a suit stood and smiled at her.

Ah, yes. The lawyer. He was probably the only person who didn't actually want to send her back to the disease-ridden jungles of Brazil.

"Ms. Suarez." He offered a wrinkly hand for a shake. "I'm Jonas Carson. Please, have a seat. I know you've had a really long day, but if you could just bear with us for a moment, we'll make this quick."

"Thank you, Mr. Carson."

"Oh, no. Jonas, please. Ginny was a good friend and spoke highly of you. I feel like I've known you for the longest." After he patted her hand, he pointed her toward a group of chairs away from the relatives from hell.

"Finally. I still don't know why we had to wait on her," an older woman complained and fanned herself with a dainty, frilly piece of silk.

Why, it was dear old Aunt Maggie Danitelli. The woman was the ultimate sourpuss and had a face to match. Sam was struck by the urge to stick her tongue out at the miserable old biddy, but she held back. She wasn't trying to start trouble, and she wasn't five years old anymore. All she wanted was for the will to be read. Then a nice, long, two-day nap sounded perfect.

Noise broke out, and complaints started to rise for her having made them wait so long. Not that she would argue with any of them. She'd been in the jungle, had traveled by every mode of transportation known to man, and was ready to chew on bark from starvation. Dios mio. Did any of those people actually think she cared what they thought? She rolled her eyes at their narcissistic behavior.

"Ladies and gentlemen." Jonas spoke over the loud complaints. "If you'll just give me a second, I'm going to pull out the last version of Mrs. Suarez's will and a video will she made. She wanted to ensure no one would fight her final wishes."

Her ass hurt so badly, all she wanted was a massage. She used a small table that stood next to her chair as an armrest. Jonas passed copies of the will to all the people in the room.

When he reached her, Jonas handed her a paper bag and gave her a conspiratorial wink. She lifted her brows and opened the bag. Oh, yes. Jonas was in the lead to be her new best friend. Inside the sack was a chicken salad sandwich, a bottle of water, and something else.

Was that... Oh god, it was! A chocolate chip cookie. She almost cried from happiness. She'd died and gone to food heaven. She pulled the food out of the bag and ate while everyone was reading the details of the will.

"As you can see from Mrs. Suarez's will, it's really all very simple..." Jonas's voice, along with all other conversation, shut off the minute Sam started to eat.

When she glanced up mid-bite, everyone had even more hatefulness to their wrinkled older faces than usual.

"How the hell does this...this..." Aunt Cecilia appeared ready to burst a blood vessel, "this girl end up with what's rightfully ours? How?" Cecilia was fuming. Red blotches covered her rounded cheeks. Her shriek reverberated through the large conference room.

Huh? Sam glanced around. What had she missed? She scanned the livid faces, each one worse than the last. If looks could kill...she'd be stabbed, beheaded, hung, shot, and probably thrown out a window. Yeah, she'd definitely missed something during her food-gasm.

Mr. Carson raised his voice. "Mrs. Suarez's will is very clear. All three of the latest versions name Ms. Samira Suarez the inheritor to the bulk of her estate. She did leave each of you one million dollars in individual accounts.

"If Samira Suarez dies within thirty days of Mrs. Suarez, each of Mrs. Suarez's female children, Cecilia, Maggie, and Luisa, would get a lump sum of twenty million dollars. Her son, Juan Senior is in the will but has been disinherited.

"According to Mrs. Suarez's will, he has his own inheritance from his father's side. Mrs. Suarez's grandchildren, Antonio, Robert, Marco, and Lucas would get ten million each and the rest would go to her designated charities."

"One million dollars!" Juan Junior jumped to

his feet. Her older cousin's face was tomato red and mottled. And that was saying something because his skin tone was a lot darker than Sam's caramel-colored flesh. The button on his collar looked ready to burst along with the seam of his pants.

"That's correct, Mr. Suarez." Jonas sounded exhausted. The poor guy must've had a hard time dealing with her horrid relatives on a regular basis. Then she noticed her grandmother's lawyer had changed since she'd left for Brazil.

Deep wrinkles lined his forehead as frown lines outlined his mouth. His suit wasn't as pressed as she remembered. Growing up, she thought he had a corn cob up his ass because he walked so straight. Then she thought the reason was his suits were so tightly pressed.

"Mi abuela — my grandma — was a billionaire, and she left us a mil a piece, but the rest to Sam?" He slapped his hands on his waist. She thought he might pull the gun he carried out of his holster and shoot her.

TWO

For the first time since she'd gotten there, a flicker of unease crawled up Sam's spine. She stopped eating, drank some water, and focused on the group.

"Mr. Carson, are you sure?" her aunt Luisa asked softly. Luisa seemed confused, but at least she wasn't actively glaring at Sam. Instead, Luisa was pale and her lips trembled as she spoke.

Luisa had always been the quiet one. She'd allowed her family to drag her into the mess of being mean to Sam, so Sam didn't really hold things against the frail woman.

"Quite sure, Mrs. Tate. If any of you dispute the will, there's a clause that automatically takes away your million dollars and gives rights for Ms. Samira Suarez to disallow anyone from using any of the properties under the Suarez Holdings."

"This can't be possible. Ginny had enough money to leave everyone at least ten million apiece and still have tons left over," added Kurt, her aunt Maggie's husband. Kurt turned to Sam, his look so chilling, it made the hairs on the back of her neck stand on end.

Sam sat there, frozen in place, watching them mull over the implications of fighting a losing battle. She, on the other hand, was just happy to be home, back to the place she'd always wanted to return to. After years of volunteering for her grandmother's favorite charity, she had no real income to call her own.

As one group, the relatives stood to depart the room. More than a few sniffed and muttered under their breaths while others ignored her and marched out.

Juan Junior stopped in front of her on his way to the door with his wife, Marcia. Junior's large belly hung over his belt. His dark face was still crimson from anger and probably high blood pressure. For a man in his early forties, she'd swear he was a heart attack waiting to happen. And with his white beard, he looked like a seething version of Saint Nick.

She lifted a brow and stood her ground. He always acted as if he were better than her and bullied her for most of her youth. Anger simmered in her blood.

"You got something you want to say to me, Junior?" Juan Junior was the biggest jerk in Black Meadows, but she wasn't intimidated. She'd grown thick skin around her family and had learned to push back.

"This isn't over, prima." His hillbilly drawl went against his sad attempt at trying to look like a businessman.

"Oh, I think it is, primo." She curled her hands into fists on her lap. "Ginny's will, all three versions, have spoken. Enjoy your inheritance and try not to waste it in one day."

She winked. Juan Junior growled. He turned and tugged Marcia out of the meeting room.

She sat, trying to calm the disappointment and anger being around the family filled her with.

Her heart jumped in her chest when Jonas pulled a chair, yanking her out of her momentary break. He sat in front of her, sighing as he lowered his body onto the wooden padded chair.

"I can see you're exhausted, so I want you to go home, rest, and if you have any questions, give me a call." He patted the hand she'd laid over one of her knees. "Ginny was a great woman. She loved you and always mentioned how proud she was you'd grown to be different than all her other children and grandchildren."

She cleared her throat. It was hard to blink away the tears that gathered in her eyes every time she thought of Grandmother Ginny. The last time she'd spoken to her, Ginny had been happy and excited that Sam was coming home soon. It was difficult to know she'd missed out on her dear grandma's last moments. Pain and pressure squeezed at her heart. If only she'd known, she'd have returned sooner.

"Thanks, Jonas. I loved her…a lot." Her voice wobbled. Ginny had been the only mother she'd ever known. She swallowed against the knot in her throat.

"I know, dear. She wanted you to have her house. And she made me promise to tell you that if you were to run into any trouble, you should call on your neighbor. I have his information around here somewhere. Give me a moment to get it for you—"

She cut him off with a negative shake of her head. "Leave it. I need some sleep, or I'm going to pass out on the floor."

"After you get settled, stop by the office sometime. I have other things for you there. Also, you should consider finding a lawyer."

She stood, her muscles screaming from exhaustion, grabbed her bags and the will packet, and followed Jonas to the door. "If you were good enough for Grandma Ginny, you're good enough for me."

Once again, she hauled her luggage while dragging her tired body out of the room.

Outside the hotel, she stopped a taxi and gave him her address. As soon as she got to the house, she dropped her bags in the living room and walked up to her bedroom.

The room was still clean and tidy, just as she'd left it before her first trip five years ago. After four years in Somalia and one in Brazil, she was finally home. Ginny had been happy to endorse the charity and support Sam's commitment to volunteering. When she'd told her grandmother she was going to teach children in the jungle how to read, Ginny had doubled the donations for that program.

She stripped off her travel clothes and opted for a shower. The next day would be soon enough to decide what the information Jonas had given her meant. When the warm spray kissed her skin, she closed her eyes and sighed.

Her thoughts drifted back to the last thing she'd done in Brazil. She'd been witness to a wedding. A man and a woman over a decade younger than Sam's twenty-seven years were joined in marriage. The couple had been so happy, and exchanges of animals and other gifts had taken place.

At that moment, she focused on the fact that she'd been alone for a really long time. Her last relationship had been years back when she'd dated another teaching volunteer in Somalia. He decided to cut his time there, and their casual relationship was over. She had stayed, and he never asked her to go with him.

Sadness and longing enveloped her, making her almost shiver with the intensity of the emotions. She donned her short-and-tank-top pajamas and threw herself onto the bed. She missed her grandmother, and her family hated her because her mother had been the black sheep. Since she had no romantic ties, she was well and truly alone. After seeing so many children and helping care for them, she realized she wanted a family of her own. What was she doing?

Sam sighed and pushed away the depression. This was not the time for a pity party. She hadn't met any men in the jungles of Brazil, but she was back in civilization now. The town of Black Meadows wasn't very big. Still, she could always call on her best friend to help her meet some people. Yes, it would work. All she had to do was try and get out there, socialize, and something might flourish. But first, she needed to polish her social skills, and Natalia, a.k.a. Nat, would help her.

As if summoned by her thoughts, her cell phone rang, and a photo of Nat's smiling face filled the screen. She placed the phone to her ear and opened a window to allow the air to circulate. While it didn't smell bad, there was staleness inside the bedroom.

"Hey, Nat." Exhaustion pulled at her, but if she ignored her best friend, she'd never hear the end of it.

"Sam, I'm so sorry I couldn't get you at the airport. I was stuck in a meeting out of town, but I'll come see you as soon as I get back the day after tomorrow." Nat's soft voice was clear across the line.

Sam sighed. "It's all right. I'm about to get some sleep. I've been traveling for twenty-four hours, and I'm exhausted."

"I'm sorry, chica. Give me a call as soon as you wake up. There are things I need to fill you in on. You've missed out on a lot while you were gone. Have you seen your neighbor yet?" Nat's voice sounded excited.

Sam yawned. Now that she'd taken a shower, she felt ready to drop. "No. I just got back from seeing the lawyer and was about to fall into bed when you called."

"Call me after you speak to him!" Nat's enthusiasm traveled through the line. "Anyway, get some rest. I'll talk to you later. I'm glad you're back safe, Sam. Te extrañe. I missed you a lot.

Video conferencing once a month is not the same as having you here."

"I know. I'm glad I'm back. I'll call you later." She shut off the phone and fell into an exhausted and blissful sleep.

THREE

She was back. Her sexy scent drifted out the open window and burrowed into Riel's heart, making him want to howl. After five long years of waiting for her to return, she was finally back. Samira. His mate.

"Yo, Ry. You still on this planet with us?" Troy's voice broke through his thoughts.

Riel turned back to Troy, who sat around the pool with the rest of their friends — all enforcers for the Black Meadows pack.

"Ry? You okay?" Kane puckered his brow. He glanced up at the window Riel had been watching, then sniffed and widened his eyes. "Is that Samira Suarez? I haven't seen her since that summer she came home from college."

Riel wanted to run to her house and take her.

She was his. She didn't know it when she left, but she belonged to him. It didn't matter that she was human. His wolf wanted her and had been waiting patiently for her return. No longer. He nodded and fisted his hands. "Yes."

Kane studied him, lifting his brows with curiosity. "What are you going to do about her? She's always been very shy of shifters. I'd swear she's afraid of our kind."

Riel knew it had to do with her mother. Samira's family was one of the few that knew about shifters because Sam's mother had been friendly with wolf shifters before she'd died. "I'll have to give her time to get to know me." How the hell he was going to do that, he had no clue.

Kane laughed. "I remember the first time you tried to talk to her. She took off before you got to say a word."

"She was young and shy," Riel grumbled. Kane continued to laugh.

Troy strode up to them. "Are we talking about Sexy Sam Suarez?"

Riel growled at Troy for the "Sexy Sam" remark. He'd had to endure their teasing since they'd realized he was infatuated with her. More like puppy love in the first degree. At least neither of them had tried to date her, or he would've had to kill them. Sam was his.

Kane sipped his beer. "Uh-huh. Remember the second time he tried to talk to her?"

"Do I? She had just come home from college. Riel, that time you got two words in before she took off like a bat out of hell, didn't you?" Troy joked.

Riel sighed. They were having fun at his expense, and he didn't like it one bit. "It was a busy time in her life. She was going off to volunteer in Somalia."

Troy slapped Riel on the shoulder. "I know. The funniest part was how you tried to puff your chest out like a big bad wolf, but that didn't help you at all. It seems to me you're going to have to tie the woman down if you ever hope to get a full sentence in around her."

Riel groaned when Sam's scent filled his lungs.

His cock hardened with just a whiff of her. He wanted her. No, he needed her. He marched back to the loungers and dropped on one of them.

It was late afternoon, and he wished his usual gathering with his friends was already over. He needed time to think, to decide on how to approach Sam without scaring her into leaving again.

Kane grinned. He sat on another lounger, leaned back, and folded his arms behind his head.

"Hey, maybe tying her up isn't such a bad idea. Some women are into that. Shit, some women beg me to tie them up."

Troy smirked. He sat on one of the stools by the outdoor bar, stretching his legs and leaning back on the counter. A bucket with ice and cold beers sat on the surface. He shoved his hand into the ice and pulled out a wet bottle.

"Yeah, most of them are also in heat, dumbass. You know when the heat strikes, they get so horny they'd hump a cactus in desperation. This is a human female. Although, I have to say she's got a fantastic body, all lush. Those curves that make men drool, and she smells great." He sniffed. "Almost like one of ours when in heat."

Riel growled and jerked up in his seat. His animal hadn't liked another male talking about his woman.

Claws pushed out of his fingers, and his canines lengthened. He eyed Troy as if he were a new threat.

"Relax, Ry." Troy lifted his hands in surrender. "I am only commenting on her scent because humans don't normally smell so...hot."

Riel blinked through the red haze of anger covering his vision. Rage pounded in his blood, jerking the wolf under the skin to break out. He clenched his jaw and spoke through gritted teeth.

"She's been in the jungle and through hell for a year. I don't want to hear another word on how hot you think she smells."

Troy opened his mouth to speak. "Ry —"

"Fucking A! I haven't even seen her yet, and I'm losing my mind." He groaned, scrubbing a hand over the back of his neck.

Kane threw a burger bun and hit Troy on the face. "Troy, you idiot. Can't you see Ry's not in the mood for your jokes? Look at him. He's hanging on to his skin by a thread."

Riel blinked, drawing deep breaths into his lungs. "It's okay."

Troy shook his head and stood. He brought Riel a beer. "Sorry, man. I didn't mean any disrespect. We've known she's yours since the moment you saw her."

Riel sighed. She was the only one who didn't know they belonged together. He'd been too concerned with scaring her in the past to try to push speaking to her or asking her out. She'd appeared so alone and vulnerable that he'd felt instantly protective of her.

Kane strode to the grill with purpose. He took the cooked meat off the fire, placing it in one of the large covered platters. He prepared a burger and sat down, then smirked at Troy. "What? Oh, was I supposed to make one for you?

Get your ass up and get it. Do I look like Mr. Belvedere or the housekeeper to you?"

Troy chuckled and threw the burger bun back at Kane. "Ry, you're starting to remind me of Chase when Sophia had the twins."

Riel laughed at that. Their alpha had turned into a softie around his wife. Whatever Sophia wanted, she got. It had been two years since they'd had to fight off hyena shifters trying to get their hands on Sophia's research.

When Sophia had the twins, Chase had turned into the ultimate protector. No one got near his wife or kids without calling him first. Sophia had smacked Chase upside the head a few times when the guys showed up with a gift for the newborns and he complained because they hadn't called ahead.

"I don't think anyone can ever be as paranoid as Chase," Kane said between bites.

FOUR

Riel picked up his beer bottle from the stone-paved ground, took a swig, and thought of Chase's position. Two children and a mate. The alpha had the ultimate blessing and knew it. No wonder he was so overprotective of his family.

Troy sat and bit into the burger he'd put together. After swallowing, he turned his attention to Riel. "Ry, what's going on with Sam Suarez? Why is she back this time? Shouldn't she be off volunteering in some country filled with mosquitoes, anacondas, and piranhas?"

Riel wished he knew. After Ginny passed, the house had been locked. The old woman had been amazing. She'd known how he felt about Sam and had asked him to wait. She promised that Sam would return to him. And now she had, but for how long?

"I'm not sure. It could be she's tired of being away and is ready to be home." God, he really hoped she was there to stay. Riel didn't think he could handle her leaving again. His patience had reached the limit.

"You're going to need some luck there. Maybe I can help." Kane prepped another burger and put a handful of potato chips on his plate, then went back to his lounger and started eating.

Riel's impatience got the best of him. "She needs time to come to terms with my wonderful personality and amazing wit," Riel joked.

Kane drank from his beer bottle. "I've been seeing Natalia Diaz," he said offhandedly.

Troy choked on his burger. He coughed and gulped down his beer. "Sam's best friend?"

Riel smiled. Troy had asked Nat out a few times only to be blatantly rejected by the redhead. She'd told him he was too much of a playboy for her to waste her time with him. It became one of the best ways to nag Troy.

Kane grinned. "Yeah. Sam's best friend. She thinks I'm adorable." He put a bunch of chips in his mouth and made loud crunching noises as he ate.

Troy's clenched jaw made Riel laugh. "So what you're saying is that you can get me inside information on Sam from Nat? And I won't have to do any crazy stunts to get her to notice me?"

Kane nodded. "And I can do it all without feeling like I'm doing you a favor because Nat is hot!"

Troy threw a pickle at Kane, and Riel laughed again. They acted like two little kids fighting over a toy.

Kane grabbed the pickle from his chest and took a bite. "What? She is hot. She's got a body that's made for loving."

Troy growled and fisted his hands. "You stay away from her body! She's mine."

"Hell no." Kane's shit-eating grin grew. "All she has to do is say the word, and I'm all hers. I don't recall seeing you claim her as yours. She's a single sexy woman with a hot body. And she likes to spend time with me. Suck on that one, pretty boy."

Riel decided to interfere before the two went to blows over Nat Diaz. The cute redhead wasn't even there and they were ready to fight for her. "How are you going to get Nat to help me?"

Kane glanced at Riel. "This is where you're going to love how friendly I am with her. She told me she wanted to make sure Sam met someone when she came home. I didn't realize she was supposed to come back so soon, but it seems she wants to play matchmaker. Who better to match

Sam with than you?"

Riel's smile widened. Excitement over the possibility of having Sam see him as more than just a shifter grew inside him. His gaze drifted back to her window. Maybe if they went on a human date, she'd be more receptive to him. It was worth a try. He needed to find a way to talk to her without scaring the shit out of her again.

FIVE

Sam woke with a start. She was drenched in sweat, hair plastered to her face. Something had disturbed her sleep. She stood and walked toward her window. The moon was out, and she had the sudden urge to strip and walk outside.

What the hell? She wondered if her brain had been damaged during her time in Brazil. She rubbed her hand over her lower calf muscle, feeling the bumps from the scar where the wolf bit her a while back. She rotated her ankle, wincing at the pull from the muscle. She'd always have the scars. Thankfully, she'd gotten every antibiotic shot known to man after it happened, and she didn't feel any different.

Next door, a man was swimming laps in his pool. Her breath caught in her chest. The pool was well lit. She openly gawked at his toned, muscled body as he sliced through the water. His powerful legs pushed him forward while his arm muscles contracted with every stroke. There was a tattoo on the man's back. It was big, but she couldn't quite make it out with all his movements.

A strange heat coursed through her body and settled in her womb. She inhaled, closed her eyes, and was shocked by what she smelled. A combination of man, fierce need, and untamed animal invaded her senses. Oh god. Something was definitely wrong with her.

What should she do? Call a doctor? A vet? A priest? A battle of wills ensued between her mind and her hormones. Her hormones won by a landslide, and she took another peek at the man in the pool.

Her nipples pebbled, her pussy clenched, and her breath hitched. He stopped swimming and glanced at her window. Panic swarmed her. She hadn't turned on the lights, and her room was enveloped in darkness. Could he see her? She hoped not.

From where he was, she made out his features clearly. Was that... Holy shit! It was him. The only man she'd ever wanted so badly, she went mute around him. Riel Karven. He was her neighbor?

His gaze was stuck on her window. And hers

was stuck on his body. His big, sexy body. She ate him up slowly as her vision roamed down his muscular torso. He'd gotten much bigger since the last time she'd seen him five years ago. Bigger and hotter.

A soft whimper slipped through her lips. He stalked toward the edge of the pool in her direction as if he were coming for her. She took hasty steps back from the window. It didn't matter that she was on the second story with a yard between them.

She continued to move away from the window until her back hit the bedroom door. For a second, it'd looked like he was going to leap up to her window and — and what?

It caught her by surprise that Riel lived next door to her. She'd been in lust with the man since she had seen him the first time when she was a teenager. If she weren't so socially inept, she might know more about him than just how hot he was. And, boy, was he hot. He was also a wolf shifter and really dangerous.

With her skin blazing a white-hot fire, she went into the bathroom attached to her room. A shower would help her...or she'd internally combust. She felt flushed under her tanned skin. Was she running a fever? Maybe she really was sick. Or maybe she was just a pervert lusting after her neighbor. Sucia! Yeah, she was a very dirty-minded girl.

After she turned on the shower, she stripped off the sweaty pajamas. When the cool water caressed her skin, she moaned at the wonderful sensation. Every pore in her body sighed in happiness. She shut her eyes, let the water drip over her head, and automatically pictured the sexy werewolf across the yard.

She panted, the sounds reverberating in the small, enclosed space. Her breathing turned erratic as air fought its way in and out of her lungs. She visualized him touching her.

The only thing filling her mind were images of his hands fondling her breasts and squeezing at her nipples. Desire rose like a wave, urging her to go next door and get him. When she glanced down, her own hands mimicked the touches he gave her in the fantasy. She whimpered.

She trailed a hand down her stomach and dipped between her thighs into her pussy lips. Fire rushed to her core. Panting and almost buckling, she drew circles over her clit, flicking on the engorged nubbin. It took an insurmountable force of will to bite down on her lip to keep from calling out to him.

Cool water kept the fire inside her under control while she played with herself. She used two fingers to pierce her sex. She squeezed at her breast and pinched her nipple hard. White spots danced before her eyes, growing wider and brighter with each thrust of her fingers into her pussy. Arousal licked at her skin. Visions of Riel biting, sucking, and taking her increased the tension in her womb.

Widening her stance, she deepened the penetration of her fingers and flicked her thumb over her clit. Breathy whimpers rushed up her throat and out of her mouth. She quickened her fingers, and then she shattered. One loud moan and her body shook.

Knees buckling, she slid down the wall until she was sitting in the tub, gasping for air. The cool water continued to rain over her heated skin. Good god. She really needed to get laid.

After she walked out of the bathroom dressed in her robe, temptation called her back to the window. Taking quiet steps, she peered through the glass to Riel's yard. There was no one there.

Movement made her turn her head. A big brown wolf ran into his yard from the woods. The animal seemed massive, his large body covered in thick, light-brown fur. He had teeth that could probably slice and dice better than her grandmother's Japanese knives. She gaped at him, wishing she were up close to see how big he really was. The wolf stopped and looked up at her window. He howled and moved toward a lounge chair.

And he shifted into one very naked, human Riel.

She gulped. His back was to her, and his perfect body flexed. Holy shit, he had the sexiest ass ever. The tattoo she'd seen on his back earlier was clearer now. A large wolf head drawn in tribal ink took over his entire back. It appeared to be staring right at her, and damn did it make her shiver. When Riel sat, she almost fell out the window. His cock was thick, long, and fully erect.

God! He lay on the lounger and stroked his cock. Well, damn. She was now a peeper and didn't give a shit. Her mouth watered, and her thoughts turned to getting down on all fours and sucking him off.

SIX

Don't stop. I want to watch you come.

As if he'd heard her thoughts, his gaze strayed back to her window. He wrapped a large hand around his cock and continued to jerk off. Beads of precum gathered at the top of his dick. He used it to lubricate his shaft and then went back to thrusting his cock into his grip. She licked at her dry lips, gawking in fascination.

His jerks increased in pace, and her breath hitched. Gripping the window ledge, she panted in unison with his jerks. He shifted until his cock was pointed to the side. Finally, he threw his head back and growled. His semen shot out, and he continued to milk his cock. Goodness. That was so hot.

His chest rose as he took a deep breath and

shot up in his seat. She stepped back in a panic, wondering if he'd seen her. Out of its own volition, her body moved to the window again. He grabbed a towel and headed to the back entrance of his house.

"Wow." If there was a nosy neighbor award, she'd definitely win it. But who the hell cared? She had just visually intruded in Riel's private self- pleasure moment and didn't even feel a little bad about it. He was hot, and she'd gladly spend another year volunteering in the jungle if it meant she'd get to have him as her form of sexual release.

* * *

Sam groaned when a loud knocking interrupted her sleep. Sunlight streamed through her open windows. She flipped to her stomach, threw a pillow over her head, and tried to ignore the incessant knocking.

When the loud yell of her name penetrated the pillow, she cursed and threw the pillow to the floor. Goddamn! She sat up in bed. Who the hell dared to mess with her sleep? Then she remembered she'd gone to bed naked. Her body had gone into overdrive after seeing Riel's private show. She'd ended up pulling out the vibrator and using it to relieve her sad, horny state.

It took some mental maneuvering, but she was able to talk her body into getting off the bed. She pulled on another set of tank-top-and-short pajamas, adding a robe over her outfit. She didn't bother fixing her messy ponytail.

Teeth brushed and mouth clean, because she didn't want to yell at anyone while there were dead soldiers in her mouth, she felt ready to face whoever was at the door. She was barefoot and in need of caffeine. She muttered her way down the stairs to the front door, going on about needing rest and sex.

"Sam!" she heard the voice yell again. Only this time she recognized it as Nat's.

She sighed and threw her door open. Within seconds, she was enveloped in a bear hug by her best friend since the third grade.

Nat took a step back and stared at her from head to toe with wide green eyes. "Oh my goodness, Samira. You look fantastic. Como—how the heck did you manage to do that while living in the jungle? How did I not see this when we did those video conferences?"

Sam rolled her eyes and laughed, ushering her friend inside. "You mean I look fat. I gained twenty—okay, probably more like thirty—pounds from eating so many carbs. My old dietician would have kittens if she knew.

"Shit, I don't even want to remember how much bread and how many green bananas I ate. Let's just say I have enough cushion on my legs, butt, and thighs to get me through a full hibernation."

Nat shook her head. "No. I mean have you seen yourself? Your normally golden skin is glowing, and you've got an even deeper tan." She snatched some of Sam's loose hair and studied the strands.

"Your hair's amazing. So shiny and gorgeous. I don't care what you say. If a woman looks as hot as you do now after a year in the jungle, then sign me up for one tour in mosquito-hell."

Sam chuckled and headed toward the kitchen. Nat shut the front door and followed behind her.

When she got to the kitchen, she went straight for the coffeemaker. "Nat, I warn you, I need coffee. You woke me up, and I'm still exhausted."

Nat sat at the kitchen table and grinned. "I'm sorry, but I had to see you. Can't you see I even cut my trip short to get my ass over here to see my best friend? I missed you like a PMSing woman misses chocolate." She pouted. "It was rough."

She giggled at Nat's silliness and set the coffeemaker. Afterward, she walked to the fridge and sent a quiet thanks to Jonas for making sure her refrigerator was stocked. Carting items to the kitchen island to make breakfast, she listened to Nat complain over how much she'd suffered without her feminine advice.

"So, have you seen your neighbor yet?" Nat asked with enough enthusiasm to rival a kid ready to go to Disney World. She bounced in her seat. Her long red ponytail swung up and down. She was clearly up to something.

"I did. It's Riel Karven."

As if unable to contain her enthusiasm, Nat stood and sprung toward her. "Isn't it fantastic?" Her eyes twinkled with excitement. "He's the guy you've had the hots for since…forever! Now you have him a few yards away. How is that not fate?" she gushed.

Sam and Nat washed their hands at the sink while they chatted. Sam started scrambling eggs for breakfast in a large skillet and shrugged. "I don't know about fate, but the guy is still able to make me freeze into stupidity."

Nat placed pieces of bacon in the same big skillet. "I think you need to be open-minded and see if things go somewhere with him. I've always had the impression he kind of liked you."

She froze for a moment. She remembered the times she'd come across Riel. He had been really nice and tried to chat with her, but she'd always taken off, afraid he'd notice she was ready to drool over him. "I don't know. I'll have to see. I just got back and still need to figure out what's going on with Ginny's estate. The entire family is ready to crucify me for getting everything."

Nat sat on one of the stools on the other side of the island. "I'm sorry, Sam. I know you loved Ginny. Were they really that bad?"

She nodded. Anger rose within her. She was starting to hate being part of that family. "You've no idea. Juan Junior looked like he wanted to take me out back and put me down like a stray dog." She placed the cooked food on platters and carted them to the kitchen table. "And you should've seen Marcia. I felt so bad for her. He left a hand print on her arm from how hard he'd grabbed her." She shook her head.

"I don't know how that woman puts up with him treating her that way. Seriously? I'd have kicked his ass and had him arrested the first time he raised his voice or his hands."

Sam was in full agreement. "I think she has issues. Ginny used to say that Marcia would always be mistreated by Juan because she was more interested in money than anything else."

"Still, would you let some man treat you like

that?"

Sam lifted a brow. "Are you out of your mind?"

Nat giggled. "I know, dumb question. You'd probably kick his ass the minute he looked at you wrong."

"I wouldn't go that far...but if you're in a relationship with someone, there has to be trust and mutual respect. Those two don't know what either of those words mean, and that's messed up because they have kids."

Her heart ached for the children Juan and Marcia had. She'd never been allowed near them because Juan openly hated her, and Marcia wouldn't dare go against what he said. "The last time I saw them they were toddlers, but I wanted to snatch them up and take them somewhere safe. Ginny said that as long as she was around, she'd ensure nothing happened to those kids, but she's gone now."

Nat set the table, brought the coffee and creamer, and took a seat. "That is a damn shame that they'd treat you that way after all these years. And to think those kids are deprived of getting to know the best teacher in the universe. Can they do something to fight the will?"

SEVEN

"Hmm, I think so, and I think some of them will try. In fact, I wish they would go ahead. I'm sick of them making it seem like I'm a leper and they shouldn't be near me." Sam said as she sat across from Nat in her grandmother's old house. "Jonas said if they fought, they'd lose their million dollars, but I don't know. He also said they'd lose all rights to the properties they are using under Ginny's estate."

She fixed a cup of coffee, took a sip, and sighed. Perfect. Now all she needed was more sleep and maybe she'd start feeling human soon.

"So they're screwed, and they're pissed at you because Ginny left them a million apiece?" Nat bit down on a slice of bacon and groaned. "Oh god. This is why I missed you. Nobody makes breakfast like you. I've been deprived. It sucks to live off cereal and toast."

Sam grinned and picked up a piece of the crunchy meat. She'd never been a fan before, but it smelled really good now. The taste exploded in her mouth. It was a salty delicious sin. Hell, she was in trouble now. She took another sip of coffee and grabbed two more pieces of bacon.

"Yeah. Can you believe it? You can feed a small country with their inheritance. It's not like that kind of money is just a few cents. And they're complaining."

"What are you going to do with Ginny's money?" Nat sucked on her greasy fingers and moaned.

Sam passed Nat a napkin and grinned when she declined, choosing instead to continue to suck the grease off her fingers.

"What she always wanted me to do. She has particular charities she wanted taken care of. That's what I'll do. Keep them going for her. I know Ginny set up her own charitable funds. But come on, I am not keeping all that money. And I'd really like to rub the family's nose in the fact they can't do anything about me giving it all away."

A warm breeze entered the large kitchen. Her thoughts were focused on what she'd need to follow-up on to set up funding for Ginny's charities. She took a deep breath and almost gagged. She scrunched her nose in distaste. "Ew. What is that stench?"

Nat bit down on a piece of bacon, visibly sniffed, and shook her head. She lifted her brows while staring at Sam. "I don't smell anything."

Sam stood and inhaled the disgusting scent again. "Yuck. It's so nasty. How can you not smell that?"

Nat scrunched her face and sniffed hard, making a loud inhaling noise through her nose. "Nope. I don't smell a thing."

Sam stepped toward the door leading to the backyard; she didn't even need to sniff anymore, the scent was overpowering. "Oh yuck. It's stronger over here."

She opened the door and glanced down. A dismembered animal was strewn on the walkway leading to the back yard. A scream tore from her throat and the food she'd eaten rolled up her throat. She gagged.

It was hard to control her stomach. She used a hand to cover her mouth and swallowed to keep from vomiting all over the entry. The smell of dead animal was unbearable.

Nat rushed over and gasped at the mutilated dog corpse. "Get back inside. You look like you're going to be sick all over the floor. Go sit down, and I'll get help." She pushed Sam inside and ran out the back door.

Sam took shallow breaths. The stench permeated the kitchen. Moments later, her back door slammed open, almost coming off its hinges. She jumped in her seat. Riel walked in wearing only a pair of shorts.

Oh good lord. What the hell had Nat done? His eyes sought her, and her heartbeat accelerated in her chest in a furious, untamed gallop.

"Sam? What's wrong? Are you okay?" He marched up to her and knelt in front of her seat.

She visually caressed him from the top of his spiky hair, down his naked torso before she remembered he had asked her a question. "It stinks really bad. Please, take it away or I'm going to be sick."

He nodded sharply, stood, and headed back out the door. She closed her eyes and focused on keeping her stomach contents still. The little bit of food she'd had was still rolling around in her gut, pushing her to let it out.

It took some mental manipulation to keep things inside. Moments later, the scent of dead animal started to dissipate. She opened her eyes to find Nat smiling at her.

"I'd say he likes you all right. All I had to do

was say your name, and he ran over before I finished the sentence." Nat strolled up to the table and took a seat across from her. She grabbed another piece of bacon and continued to eat.

Nat grinned. "We are not wasting perfectly good food. Besides, I don't smell anything. You've got some keen sense of smell. I don't remember you ever doing that before."

She was about to answer when the door opened again. Riel walked inside with a tall blond guy. Wow. He looked like a really hot version of Thor. And somewhat familiar. Of course, he had nothing on her spiky-haired, sexy neighbor. Only Riel made her drool and pant at the same time. She shook her head at herself.

When Nat huffed, she glanced at her friend.

Nat's face was set into her don't-fuck-with-me expression.

Riel pointed to the blond and headed to the kitchen sink. "Sam, this is Troy Helix. He's also an enforcer for the Black Meadows Pack." He washed his hands at her sink as he spoke. Once he was done, he walked back to Troy.

Oh. Another shifter. She'd stayed away from shifters all her life because they seemed so large and dangerous. Now she had two in her house like it was no big deal. The interesting thing was that Troy had locked his gaze on Nat and hadn't glanced away from her once.

Nat's face had turned a telling shade of red. Aha. Something was definitely going on with those two.

"Troy? Haven't we met before?" She stood and shook the hand he offered.

Troy smiled, firmly shook her hand, and stepped back next to Riel. "We have, but it's been years. Nice to see you back in town, Sam." He looked back and forth between the two women. "So can someone tell us why there would be a dead animal at your back door like a sick welcome home gift?"

"If we knew that, we would've told you already, Casanova. Sam doesn't know why some weirdo would've left that at her door." Nat pursed her lips and folded her arms over her chest.

Riel stepped toward Sam, giving her one of those sexy grins she remembered, the ones that made her go mute and run like a bat out of hell. "Can I speak to you alone for a moment?"

EIGHT

Sam glanced back and forth between the other couple, wondering if it was a good idea to leave them alone. Nat knew how to take care of herself, but it was Troy she was worried about. Her friend would tear him a new one if he pissed her off. She nodded and headed toward the living area with Riel.

Electricity buzzed over her skin. The man she'd always had a crush on was in her house. It seemed almost unreal. Her thoughts bounced back and forth between running back to the safety of the kitchen or following her hormones and throwing herself at Riel.

When she reached the living room, she stopped and turned. Her breath hitched in her throat at his proximity. Jesus. The man even walked like a predator.

Too preoccupied with the other couple not killing each other, the dead animal at her doorstep, and the crazy arousal running rampant inside her, she hadn't even heard him get as close as he had. She inhaled and whimpered.

Horrified, she took a step away from him. A slow smile spread over his sexy lips. Don't mentally strip him. Don't mentally strip him. Too late. Her mind went back to the images of him jerking off the previous night. Oh lord. She was so going to hell. There just wasn't enough prayer in the world to save her soul when the only thing flashing through her mind were images of her doing really dirty things to him.

"What—" she cleared her throat, "what did you want to discuss?" She made a beeline for a sofa chair. He sat on a matching larger sofa across from her.

Tension increased in the room the longer he sat there saying nothing. What the hell was he thinking?

Probably much more normal things than the perverted thoughts doing cartwheels in her mind.

Thank god he wasn't a mind reader, or he'd know she was licking every inch of his sexy body in a daydream. She wished she could just tell him to strip for her. She mentally cheered him to take it all off.

Shake what your mama gave you, you sexy thing.

His voice broke through the fantasy strip show. "You can look all you want, darling." He grinned.

She blinked and swallowed. Was he flirting with her? "Sorry, I didn't mean to stare..." Liar! Yes, she did. "You just seem bigger than the last time I saw you."

Her body throbbed. How did his scent arouse her girl parts faster than any man had in her life?

More of his white teeth made an appearance. A sexy dimple showed in his cheek, and he winked. He was definitely flirting. "Like I said, I don't mind. If you want more than that, I'm willing to accommodate you. I've been waiting for you to want to do more than look for a long time, Samira."

What? Sam had to bite her tongue to keep from ordering him to strip down to nothing. "Uh, thanks."

He glanced at her mouth. She traced the muscles rippling in front of her with her eyes and her temperature shot out of orbit. Oh, but she was in definite trouble. She was ready to jump on his lap and ride him. What in the world was wrong with her?

"I know you just got back from a long stint of volunteer work. Are you planning on staying here long-term?"

Surprised at the amount of information he knew about her, she raised her brows and nodded. "I am. My five years are over. That was my goal and promise to Ginny. I achieved it; I'm done. My goal was to do something to give back before I came home to teach locally. I'm here to stay."

"Have you had any problems with anyone that would cause them to leave that kind of surprise by your door?"

She thought of her relatives. At any other time, she'd take their attitude as the norm, but since he was asking. "Well..."

"What?" he pressed, the smile sliding off his handsome face. "Anything you can think of is important in finding out who did it."

"When they did the reading of Ginny's will, I was named the sole inheritor, and it created some tension among my other relatives." She bit her lip and rubbed her hands over her robed knees. "They're not very happy with me right now. Let me rephrase that, they've never been happy with me, only right now, it seems they hate my guts more than usual." She almost jumped out of her skin when he growled.

His voice turned raspy and so deep, it was hard to make out what he said. "Have any of them threatened you?"

Sam shook her head. The need to pacify him blossomed inside her. He sat stock-still, but angry energy vibrated off him, seeping into her pores and turning up her anxiety. It didn't feel right. She wanted him laughing again.

"No. No one threatened me. They were more upset that they didn't get more money, but no one made any remarks to make me feel like my life was hanging by a thread. Besides, I can take care of myself."

He slid to the edge of his seat and curled one of his hands over hers. "I won't let anything happen to you. You don't have to worry. No one will hurt you." The conviction in his voice made something soft work its way into her heart.

"Thank you. I don't really think anyone means me harm. It's probably just a prank. I've been gone for a while, but I know there are still teenagers all over this town. They love doing things like this."

"They do not love dismembering dogs, Sam."

"Yeah, okay. But I still say it was just a one-time prank." Saying the words and believing them were two different things. But this was her family. They had been jerks to her forever, but no one had done anything to make her think they wanted her dead. Though now they had billions of reasons to want her dead.

He drew circles over her palm with the tip of his finger. A low heat gathered in her stomach, growing with every little twirl, and pooled at her core. Oh god. Not now. His eyes darkened to a molten gold. She'd never seen anything as beautiful.

Her breath hitched. She stared at his dilating pupils until there was only a small rim of gold visible. The fire in her veins roared. Her gaze slid down until it fastened on his lips. She darted her tongue over her dry lips, glanced up, and caught him staring at her action with unwavering interest.

"Sam…" His gravelly voice sent shards of electricity straight to her nipples. The buds tightened into hard little nubs begging for his touch.

She felt as if an invisible pull existed between them, so thick and strong, she could almost touch it. "I don't…know what you're doing to me…"

She blinked. In the time it took her to take a breath, he tugged her out of her seat and placed her sideways over his lap. His cock was long, hard steel under her butt, rubbing and poking her between her thighs. He wanted her. Lust skittered down her spine and settled in her pussy.

"I need you, Sam. I've been waiting so long for you."

NINE

Emotions expanded inside Sam's heart, emotions of belonging and yearning she wasn't familiar with.

Words she never expected to say rolled off her tongue. "I want you."

Excited butterflies took flight in her chest, dipping and diving at the look of pure possession in his eyes.

He cupped her face, caressed her cheek, and pressed his lips over hers hard, devouring her with the intensity of his kiss. So much passion came through when their lips met, it made oxygen vanish from her lungs.

He stroked her jaw and pulled her closer into him. Every swipe of his tongue ratcheted up the inferno in her blood. Her pussy clenched, and her shorts drenched with her need. She whimpered in the back of her throat, ran her nails into the short spikes of his hair, and fisted tightly. Arousal coursed through her and urged her to get him naked.

Everything ceased to exist but the amazing things he was doing to her. She rocked her hips over his cock and moaned when he rubbed her swollen folds. He slid a hand under her robe and up her shorts. Her breath reeled in her chest, squeezing its way into her lungs. One quick moan and he was spreading her pussy lips with his fingers and gliding two digits into her sex.

"Oh god." Moans rolled up her throat between kisses as she lolled her head to the side. He sucked, licked, and nipped her jaw and throat, turning her into an incoherent pile of nerves.

"Sam…" She wiggled on his hand. "Baby, you're so wet. God, I never knew you'd be this hot, this responsive to my touch. Do you like it when I do this?" He curled a finger in her pussy and rubbed her G-spot.

She shuddered. "Oh lord. I love it." She ground her hips into his hand. More. She wanted to come.

He licked the shell of her ear. "Shh. They're going to hear us in the kitchen."

What did he say? Her mind went blank. She

spread her legs wide over his and leaned back into him. She ended up draped over him like a blanket.

He continued to slide in and out of her pussy in lazy, short drives. Meanwhile, he moved his other hand under her shirt, trailed up her stomach until he reached one of her breasts, and squeezed. She whimpered.

Her body begged for harder penetration, for the feel of his cock inside her, and for his body branding hers. Need and hunger for him made her ache. She'd never experienced this kind of desperation before. She might have been scared if her hormones hadn't taken over her thinking and overridden all thoughts not centered on her lusty needs. Her legs shook, and her pussy grasped at his digits.

"Yes," she whimpered. "Please, Ry. Make me come."

"I'll make you come so hard, you'll never want me out of your sight again." His deep voice made the blood thicken in her veins. He tweaked her nipple again, harder. He thumbed her clit, and his teeth grazed her shoulder in small nibbles. Tension gathered inside her.

He turned rougher, growling softly by her ear at the same time he dominated her with his hands. He fondled her other breast and pinched her clit with two fingers.

Once she was at the edge of an ecstasy free fall, he bit into the back of her neck, and she shattered. He covered her mouth just as she came, muffling her loud groan while waves of pleasure rushed through her body. Her pussy sucked at his fingers as he continued to drive the digits in and out of her sleek sex. She panted, taking big gulps of air. What the hell just happened?

She lay limply over Riel. It was going to take more than a minute to figure out how she'd gone from talking to him to having a mental shutdown and her body overtaken by lust.

She really needed to get laid. He shifted her so she was now sideways on his lap again. He rubbed up and down her spine. If she hadn't felt so fulfilled, she'd be highly embarrassed right now, but something about Ry soothed her nerves. She burrowed her face into his neck and inhaled his scent. Another wave of lust shot through her.

Alarmed, she lifted her head. "What the hell is wrong with me?"

"What do you mean?"

"I've never felt so…so needy in my entire life." She sat up and turned her upper body fully on his lap to face him, his hard cock still poking at her ass. "It's like my body is demanding all the sex I haven't had in years!"

His brows lifted, and a wide grin spread on

his lips. "Years? Baby, don't worry, I'll make it so good for you, it'll be like you never left."

Oh lord. Did she just admit to not having sex to the sexiest man alive? Talk about sounding desperate.

"Cut it out. You sound like an advertisement for desperate women, which is exactly how I feel after saying what I said."

"You would never be desperate in my eyes, Sam. You're a very special woman."

She licked her lips and continued to study his handsome face while tracing the muscles of his shoulder with the pads of her fingers. "I...I have always been attracted to you."

Why she felt the need to confess, she didn't know, but it seemed like the right moment with the open concern he showed.

"I'm much more than attracted to you, Sam.

You're—"

TEN

A loud bang sounded from the kitchen, and she jumped off his lap as if she'd been bitten by a snake. She rushed to fix her robe.

Running shaky fingers through her messy hair, she tried to compose herself. Another louder, noise came from the other room, and she hurried to where she'd left Nat and Troy. She expected to find blood littering the floor and body parts strewn all over the room. What she hadn't expected was for Nat and Troy to be groping like two teenagers on their first make-out session.

Riel chuckled behind her and wrapped an arm around her waist. He cleared his throat loudly. She glanced up, and he winked at her. She gaped at the humor twinkling in his eyes. Heat crawled across her skin, and she tried to move out of the kitchen to give the other couple privacy. His grip on her waist tightened.

"Troy, you done interviewing Nat's tonsils?" Riel joked.

Nat jerked away from Troy. Sam's curiosity over the two was beyond piqued. Why hadn't Nat mentioned Troy in any of their video calls? Hell, the way it looked, if they were given any more time, she definitely would have walked in on some private playtime.

Troy stared at Nat as if she was a porkchop and he was meat deprived. "I think we can continue this later on. Don't you, sweetheart?" He grinned.

Nat sat on one of the stools in a huff. "Have you lost your mind? I already told you I don't want anything to do with a playboy like you."

Troy gave her a shit-eating grin. "Sweetheart, you don't just want me." He licked his lips. "You want me so badly, you were ready to tear at my clothes a few moments ago."

Nat rolled her eyes. "Oh please! That was just a moment of temporary insanity."

They argued back and forth. It shocked her. Sam grinned when she realized why her friend was so prickly with Troy. Nat wanted the sexy blond but refused to give in to her hormones. Boy, she was in for some long, battery-operated nights.

"Since I can't show Sam what a great catch I am with you two arguing, how about you behave for a few minutes and we get back to the problem at hand here?"

Sam peeked up at Riel. He was grinning at the couple while the bar of his really hard cock pressed against her ass. She wiggled until the thick length was nestled between her cheeks. Maybe she could find a way to ask Troy and Nat to leave so she could get better acquainted with him.

Riel's head dropped, his voice low by her ear. "If you keep doing that, I will drag you upstairs, tear off your clothes, and lick you until you come. Then I'm going to fuck you so hard, you'll be limping for days."

Good god! The visual he'd given her sent her temperature soaring. She'd never known he was such a dirty talker, and dammit she liked it. She wanted to be upset with him for interrupting the live soap opera in her kitchen, but her thoughts were all in the gutter, way in the gutter, so deep down there you'd need a flashlight to find them.

It was better to watch Nat argue with Troy than to delve into what just happened in her living room. She would take anything over dissecting how she'd let Riel fondle her just steps from them and how badly she wanted him to continue what he'd started.

She strode toward the table and sat next to the cold food. Hunger pangs made her stomach grumble. She ignored the noise her gut made and focused on the conversation, her gaze straying back to Riel.

He'd moved into the kitchen and was actively washing his hands, hands that had been all over her body just moments before. She gulped. He turned, winked at her, and grabbed a bag of sliced bread off the kitchen counter.

"Troy, you look into the teenagers around the area. See if any of them might know if this was some kind of prank." Riel placed the bread in the toaster.

Troy gathered the dirty dishes and loaded them into the dishwasher.

The toast popped out with a ding. Riel grabbed the dark slices and buttered them. She glanced at Nat, who was grinning over both men's domesticity. Sam was much more interested in figuring out what Riel was up to, acting like her kitchen was his personal domain. Not that she minded.

Hell, any man who knew how to cook and was as sexy as Riel was more than welcome in her home. And if she got him out of his pants, all would be well in the world.

Riel pushed the plate of buttered toast off to the side. He opened a carton of eggs on the counter and broke them into a bowl. He mixed them with a fork, his naked arm muscles shifting with each movement, drawing Sam's attention to his sexy back.

The wolf tattoo was even more amazing up close. He turned to face her, moving the bowl by the skillet. "I'll look into the relative connection."

"What relatives?" Troy asked, pulling juice out of the fridge.

"The ones that may or may not have something to do with the dead animal left outside." He cooked the eggs and glanced up, his piercing gaze meeting Sam's eyes. "Ginny's will left everything to Sam, and they're angry. I'll have a look into what might be going on there."

Sam wondered if Riel and Troy forgot they were in her house. Interest had replaced shock that they were cooking. She waited to see what each would do next. Riel placed bacon in a frying pan, and Sam's stomach growled louder. Troy made fresh coffee, and Nat cleared the table. Meanwhile, she just sat there, like a moviegoer watching the latest suspense flick, unable to move.

Nat shrugged and grinned at Sam's most likely dumbfounded expression before placing clean cutlery on the table. She added her two bits into the conversation. "Those people were always so miserable. All they've ever wanted is Ginny's money."

"I know." Riel scooped the food onto two large platters. "She told me often enough that she wished she could disinherit them all and start over."

Sam thought Ginny must've felt comfortable with Ry. She glanced up when he placed a plate piled with breakfast in front of her.

"Eat." He had that really hot, panty-melting smile and sat next to her. As if in agreement, her stomach grumbled.

It was still surreal that he'd cooked for her. A warm, soft feeling settled into her heart. Could it be possible things were looking up for her in the personal-life front, except for that dead dog issue?

Maybe she was finally being noticed and wanted by the man she'd been gaga over since she was a kid. The latter sounded good to her.

ELEVEN

Riel and Troy left together. Once they were back inside his home, Riel turned to his friend. "We need to figure out why that dead animal was left at Sam's door. My gut tells me this was no prank."

Troy pulled out his cell phone and pressed keys as he spoke. "I agree. It was dismembered, not just dead. And that shows viciousness we don't want to see from anyone. I'm sending a message to have Kane and Zeno check into any previous boyfriends or relationships as well."

Riel snarled. "She doesn't have anyone. She's been alone for years."

Troy nodded. "I understand, but we don't really know anything other than Sam has been away for five years. What if she picked up a stalker who volunteered with her at that time? We need to make sure. There's too much we don't know that we need to find out."

Riel headed to the back yard. He knew Troy made sense, but to think of Sam with anyone else made his blood boil. She was his mate, and no one would lay a hand on her again.

He stripped off his clothes and let the wolf free. Troy followed suit behind him. They pawed at the ground around her back yard where the dead dog had been lying. Riel dug his claws into the dirt, taking deep whiffs as he went. He was still able to communicate through his wolf with Troy.

"She told me she's been with no one in years." Riel sniffed the ground. He tried to find anything scenting different than the rotting smell the dead dog gave off.

"Years? That's surprising. She's beautiful." Troy sniffed as well.

Riel stopped and glanced up at Sam's window. "Yes. I'm not letting her go this time. She's here to stay, and I'm keeping her by my side."

"Don't you think she has a say?" Troy chuckled. "I mean from what Nat keeps saying, women aren't won over by being told what to do. She's very loud about reminding me of that."

Riel pictured the scene on Sam's sofa. She'd come apart in his arms, and there had been enough heat in her eyes to make him want to beg her to let him make her his. "Hell no. She's made her choice. If her body's response is any indication, she wants me. I'm not waiting another five years. She's here now, and that's how it's going to stay."

Troy growled, and Riel moved to the spot his friend crouched.

"It smells sweet," Troy complained. "Like an overripe fruit."

There were no fruit trees in Sam's yard. Riel sniffed at the spot. "It's not fruit. It's perfume. A fruity type of perfume or maybe a body spray."

Leaves crunched under their paws with each step they took, the sound louder to their sensitive animal ears. Once they returned to his yard, they shifted, dressed, and sat by the pool.

The lines of Troy's face pulled tight with concern. "I think there's more here than just a prank, Ry."

Riel thought of the sweet fragrance and memorized it. Something about it didn't sit right. Women wore scents like that, but what woman would leave a dead dog for Sam? The ringing of his cell phone pulled him out of his musings. Sophia's name lit his screen.

He grinned and answered quickly. "Sophia, you sexy woman. When are you going to leave that ogre you call a mate and run away with me?" Sophia was one of his favorite people. She was a little crazy and so much fun.

"I'm seriously considering it, Ry. Even if it's just so I can get some sleep." She laughed.

She sighed, which worried him. "Are you okay? The twins?"

Her chuckle sounded across the line. "Yes. You sound just like Chase. Actually, the reason I'm calling is because I'm coming over with Shane and Selena. I want to talk to you about something."

Riel's brows lifted in surprise. Normally Sophia asked him to come to her, not the other way around. "Does Chase know you're coming this way?"

She laughed again. "Of course. Do you think he'd just sit by while I took off with the kids without knowing where he could find us? He'd come chasing after us to make sure we're okay. I don't need that kind of stress in my life.

"Two fifteen-month-old twins trying to climb over everything are enough to keep any person on the brink of insanity. Not that I ever claimed to be sane. Anyway, we'll see you in a bit. I just wanted to make sure you were home."

The line went dead before he got a chance to say anything else. He chuckled. Ever since the hyena episode two years back, Sophia said he was her new adopted brother. She always made sure to find out what he was up to and bring him to family gatherings.

She and her sister, Julia, loved calling on him for all kinds of favors. Their favorite was for him to babysit while they went shopping, but he didn't mind. Especially when he got to spend time with all the kids. Shane, Selena, and Jasen were his favorite kids. There was never a dull moment when those three were nearby.

"Sophia, huh?" Troy grinned.

Everyone got a kick out of her. She had gone from quiet scientist to outspoken leader in the blink of an eye. They loved watching her when she got big pack Alpha Chase to do whatever she wanted without batting a lash.

Riel nodded. "Yeah. She's coming this way. Says she wants to discuss something."

Troy laughed. "Uh-oh. It sounds like you're going to be babysitting again. How much shopping can those two women do?"

Riel headed toward his kitchen. "I don't know, but I can tell you this. There's one room in each of their houses dedicated to shoes. Only shoes. I don't understand why all the shoes. They can only wear one pair at a time, but they must have a collection. It's scary." He pulled two soda cans out of his fridge and threw one to Troy.

"Yeah." Troy smirked. "Just wait until you figure out what Sam's weird shopping joy is."

Riel thought back. Ginny never mentioned Sam having a preference for shopping sprees. "I don't think she has one."

Troy gulped down the soda. "Trust me, she has one. They all have something they like to buy. Shoes, clothes, bags, hats, books, trinkets, etcetera. I don't know why, but they love to buy stuff."

TWELVE

Riel doubted all women had that. Sam didn't seem like the type to spend mindless hours shopping. But if she did like shopping, he had more than enough space in his house for all the shoes she wanted to buy.

Troy dumped the empty soda can in the recycling bin. "I'm going to check on the teens around the area. You have fun with the little ones. Don't think I don't know you love being surrounded by babies. I've never met a man that liked kids as much as you."

"Don't hate. You're just jealous because they like me better." Riel laughed and pushed his friend out the front door. So what if he liked kids. Until he had some of his own, he could enjoy Shane and Selena.

"I'm not jealous." Troy flushed and step off the porch.

Riel stood by the door, laughing and watching Troy cross the street to his own house. A large hybrid SUV he recognized as Sophia's turned into his driveway. He jogged to her vehicle and opened the back door to pull out Selena.

The little girl squealed and started chanting, "My Ry Ry."

"That's right, princess. I'm all yours." He grinned and hugged the girl's little body tightly. Her short brown curls had escaped her pigtails and her gray eyes twinkled with mirth.

Holding the little girl in his arms, he went around the car and allowed Sophia to give him a kiss on the cheek. She was losing weight. Her cheekbones were more prominent than before and shadows marred her eyes. "Are you okay? You look exhausted."

She grinned and strolled into his house. They headed straight for the backyard where he always had a playpen for the kids. Sophia placed Shane in the portable playpen and took a seat on a lounger next to it.

"I'm fine. Nothing a few months of sleep won't cure. I guess I'll have to hire a nanny in order to get some rest with this pregnancy."

Riel had been bouncing Selena on his lap and stopped. He grinned and stood to give her a hug. "Congratulations. I am guessing Chase is going to turn into an even bigger paranoid papa?"

Sophia laughed and sat back down. "He downloaded an app to my phone so we could see where the other was every minute of the day. His reasoning was in case I went into labor somewhere on the road, I'd know where he was. I think it's more like he'd know where I am every minute of the day."

Riel studied her face. "Wow. Definitely paranoid. Okay. What do you need from me?"

"Actually, it's what you need. You need help. I'm here to offer it."

He groaned. He hoped she wasn't going where he thought. "What? What help?"

Sophia chuckled when he attempted a pout.

Selena, noticing his pout, grabbed hold of his bottom lip and pulled. "Come on, Ry. You told me about Samira, remember? I know she's back. So I have an idea."

Uh-oh. Sophia looked like she was going to make it her business to get Riel and Sam together.

He kissed Selena's neck, and the little girl giggled, smacking his cheeks with her chubby hands.

Riel was afraid to ask but had to know. "Okay, fine. What's your idea?"

"A barbeque." She grinned. "It's really easy. We'll have a huge gathering, and you'll bring her with you, and she'll see how awesome you are with the kids. Trust me, that is a major wow factor with women."

Riel wondered if Julia would come over later with her own ideas on how to get him and Sam together.

Sophia glanced at the house across the yard. To his surprise, Sam's gaze was fixed on him and Selena. There was softness in her eyes and a wistful smile on her face.

"Then again we might not need to do anything after all." Sophia stood and headed toward Sam's yard.

His alpha's mate introduced herself to Sam.

"Hi. I'm Sophia Blackburn. Would you like to join us? I promise not to bite, although I can't guarantee my kids won't. They're still going through the wanting-to-gnaw-on-everything-they-see phase."

Sam shook Sophia's hand as indecision rushed across her face. When Selena blew bubbles, Sam nodded and quickly made her way toward his yard. As she neared, she caught sight of Shane and squealed. Complete adoration covered her face.

"They're twins! What a handsome little boy. They are so cute." Sam turned to Sophia. "May I hold him?"

Sophia grinned and sat next to the playpen. "Knock yourself out. As much as I want to hold them both all day, my arms get kind of tired. He's Shane, and the little princess in Ry's arms is Selena."

Sam picked up Shane, and the little boy stared at her for a long moment.

"Hi, Shane. I'm Samira. Can you say Sam?" She stared at the child, fascinated. "You are the cutest little boy I have ever seen." Shane appeared instantly won over, because he grabbed handfuls of her hair and pulled her head down. Then he sniffed her cheek and said, "Sam."

Riel pictured Sam with their own children. She cooed and bounced Shane.

Sophia sniffed and raised her brows, glancing pointedly at Riel. He had no idea what she scented. Her sense of smell had developed into a lethal weapon since she'd gotten pregnant the first time around.

"Sam, what do you do?" Sophia asked.

Riel could see the wheels turning in her head.

Sophia's scientific mind was a dangerous thing.

Sam sat on a lounger and bounced Shane on her lap. She caressed the little boy's face with so much affection, one would think it was her child. "I'm a teacher."

"And I understand you were volunteering?" Sam glanced at Sophia, who was smiling at Shane's antics; the boy was tugging on Sam's hair. "I met Ginny, and she loved speaking highly of you."

Sam nodded. "Yes. I was in Brazil this past year and in Somalia before that. I'm back now."

"To stay, I presume?"

"Yes. I... It's time to be home." She sighed.

"So, tell me about Brazil? It sounds exotic." Sophia asked with enough enthusiasm that Sam wouldn't know she was being interviewed. Only Riel could see right through what she was doing.

"Not really. I taught kids and adults in the Amazon. In fact, the most interesting thing that happened while I was down there was me getting bitten by a stray wolf."

"What?!" Sophia and Riel yelled at once, startling the young one.

Riel glanced down at Selena. She pouted, her eyes filling with tears. "I'm sorry, sweetheart. I didn't mean to scare you."

Sam continued to grin at Shane and answered, "Oh, it was nothing. I got all kinds of tests and vaccinations. Let's just say there's not a single bug inside my body that could have resisted all the medication I was given."

Sophia glanced at him. She bit her lip and widened her eyes to give him a silent signal. He knew exactly what she was wondering. Was that a regular wolf or a wolf-shifter? Her blood would need to be tested. A lump formed in his throat. She didn't appear to be sick or going through the change. That pacified him somewhat.

Sophia continued her inquisition. "Sam, do you have any shifters in your family?"

Riel wondered why she asked that question. Sam and her relatives were human. She scented human to him. He continued to watch Sam rock Shane in her arms. The little boy's head drooped to her shoulder, and his eyes closed.

Sam's voice was soft when she replied. "No. None that I've ever heard of. I understand my mom was friends with some, and that made her the black sheep of the family."

Sophia sniffed delicately. "You're sure? Maybe they missed someone."

Sam shook her head. "No, I would know. Ginny wouldn't have kept that kind of information from me. She was always very open about our family and the type of people we had as a part of it. She always said we had some rude excuses for adults, but never mentioned any shifters."

Riel ate up the scene of Sam holding little Shane and smiling down at him. She nuzzled the little boy's soft curls and sniffed. A smile curled her lips. Every possessive cell in his body roared. He wanted to take her to bed and fill her with his seed until she carried his own children. Heat traveled across the space between them. It ran down his body and made him desperate to have her.

THIRTEEN

Sam was in love. Shane was the cutest little boy she'd ever encountered, and she'd encountered many a cute baby. Selena could be a duplicate for a little doll.

Sam's hormones were going crazy with both babies in sight. The famous biological clock she'd always heard of was making its presence known, big time. It was avidly hammering the point that she was of an age where she could bear children.

Hell, it was pretty much smacking her upside the head and telling her to get a move on. Her gaze strayed back to Sophia Blackburn. The Black Meadows alpha's mate. Shifter.

When she'd first seen her in Riel's yard, a stab of jealousy had hit her. She almost ran over to the other woman to demand she state her business with Ry. Her heart flipped with emotions she'd never had this early in any relationship, especially not after one day.

It was unreal and completely insane. And yet it felt perfectly normal. But then she'd seen Riel holding the little girl, and she'd gotten all kinds of visions of him with their baby. The man gave her one amazing orgasm, and here she was ready to marry him and have his kids. It was a good thing he couldn't look inside her head, or he'd be running a million miles in the other direction.

Smiling at the baby, she thought of how badly she'd been feeling the need for her own family. She glanced up at Riel, and her heart constricted. He was smiling at her with so much warmth, she wanted to tear off his clothes, then and there, and beg him to make her his. Sophia's voice broke through her vision.

"I should get going before Chase starts calling me and asking if I'm feeling fine." Sophia jiggled Selena from Riel then turned to Sam. "Would you mind just walking him to the car with me? I hate to move them when they're asleep just to go from hand to hand."

"Of course." Sam followed behind Sophia and Riel into the front yard. She laid the sleeping boy in his car seat. Too tempted to hold back, she gave him a kiss on the forehead. Then she ran a finger down his chunky cheek. Her heart melted when the baby cooed in his sleep.

She stepped back and found Riel and Sophia staring at her. Sophia had that motherly pride look, the one that said she knew her children were beautiful and wanted the world to see them.

Meanwhile, Riel was so possessive, warmth settled on Sam's cheeks and fire coursed through her blood.

Once Sophia was gone, she and Riel walked into his house. They stopped in the kitchen, and he offered her a drink.

He rummaged through the fridge. She stood there, drinking in the vision of his muscular body, flexing with every move he made, taunting her to touch him. He was so hot.

Electric currents darted down her veins and settled in her pussy. She opened her mouth to take a much-needed breath, but a soft moan escaped. She gulped, widening her eyes.

Riel slammed the fridge shut and spun toward her in light speed. His nose flared, and he inhaled deeply. His eyes turned a molten gold again. She now knew it meant he was aroused. Moisture gathered between her thighs and dripped to her panties.

"Sam." The gravelly rumble made her nipples ache.

She took a shallow breath as her gaze

roamed his face, down his body, and then slowly back up to his flared nostrils. He stepped closer, and she whimpered. Oh lord. What the hell was wrong with her? Every hormone in her system begged for him. Wanted him. Needed him.

"Riel, I..."

Her throat went dry. He stalked toward her, watching her with enough possession to make the hairs on her arms stand on end. He focused on her mouth. She swiped her tongue over her dry lips, and his eyes darkened, the specks of amber turning brighter by the second.

He stopped in front of her, wrapped his hands around her waist, and hauled her into him. She sniffed at his neck and flicked her tongue over his throat. The burst of untamable flavor made her moan.

He tasted of wilderness, raw animal lust, and of some elusive musky flavor that made her pussy throb. Her panties soaked with her wet heat. She'd never been so ready to drop all her inhibitions for a man before. She lifted her face to his, and their mouths met in a frantic mating. He didn't as much kiss as he possessed. He conquered her with his tongue, rubbing the inside of her mouth with enough passion, she thought she'd burst into flames.

The world shifted, and she was scooped into his arms. As he walked up the stairs with her, she ran her hands into his short brown hair, kissing his throat and licking at the pulse beating erratically under her tongue. She grazed her blunt teeth over his neck and nipped at the warm flesh. He groaned and dropped her on the bed.

"Tell me now if you don't want this." He gave her a heated look.

She got on her knees on the bed as lust shot through her. He clenched his jaw. Gripping the sides of her tank top, she lifted it above her head and flung it at him after she took it off.

His gaze darted to her satin-covered breasts. She moved a hand to the hook on her back and unclasped her bra, all the while watching his eyes sparkle like liquid gold.

He was seeking her consent even when he was clearly having a hard time holding himself back from pouncing on her. The thought of him fucking her wildly made her pussy flutter again. She licked her lips and moved her hands to her shorts.

"Stop." The growl was almost unintelligible. She knew what he needed. "Please, Riel." "Tell me." His voice made the fire in her blood

blaze.

"I want you, Ry. Now. Right now." Flames licked at her skin.

"You're sure?"

What happened to the man offering her all kinds of orgasms just that morning? "I've never wanted anyone the way I want you right now."

She panted while he ripped off his clothes in hurried movements. The sound of tearing cloth enhanced her arousal, thickening her blood in her veins. There was her wild man.

He marched to the bed, his powerful legs flexing with each step. His cock stood proud, pointing up to his belly button. Oxygen levels depleted in her lungs the longer she stared at his thick shaft.

Pre-cum oozed from his slit, sliding down the sides of his long length. Passion overran every other thought in her brain. She needed him. Their lips met in a desperate kiss, and she whimpered in joy. She splayed her hands over the warm, muscled flesh of his chest as her pussy throbbed and begged to come.

He cupped her breasts and squeezed the aching mounds. Rolling the twin tips between his fingers, he brought her to the edge of sanity. He nibbled her neck, her lips, and traveled down until he latched on to a nipple.

FOURTEEN

Her breath caught, and she saw stars. He slid his hands down her body, to her shorts, and shoved them down her legs, while flicking his tongue over one swollen nipple. She moaned. Every touch was a silken caress on her heated skin. He detached from her nipple and pushed her to lie back on the pillows on the bed. The shorts came off, along with her panties.

He sat on his heels, his gaze dark, piercing, and possessive. Her breath reeled. She lay there, completely naked and spread eagle, uncaring how she looked. Desire and arousal shut down any wariness within her. Only thoughts of him filling her until the ache inside her womb ceased swarmed her.

She breathed shallow gulps of air, fighting to clear the haze of lust overpowering her mind.

Small flames kissed every place his gaze touched on her body.

"So beautiful. I'm going to eat you up until all your honey drips on my tongue. Then I'm going to make you come — and you will come — on my mouth," he promised in a husky voice.

She bunched the comforter in her fists. He kissed her foot. Harsh moans struggled past her lips as arousal skyrocketed inside her. He licked, kissed, and nibbled up her foot, to her knee, up her thigh until he stopped a hairsbreadth from her pussy. She moaned. Each of his caresses felt like a flutter of warmth over her skin.

He lowered onto his belly and flashed golden eyes at her. Arousal had tightened his features into rigid lines and severe angles. Goodness, the man was even sexier with that wild, about-to-lose-control look. He pushed her legs apart, making room for his large, bulky shoulders, and wrapped his arms around her thighs. His hot breath stroked her heated folds. She almost came off the bed when he buried his nose into her sex.

"Mine." He growled into her pussy lips. The vibration was enough to send shards of pleasure up her spine.

"Oh god." She moaned and rocked her hips over his lips.

He licked a slow trail around her entrance and up her clit. Each swipe ratcheted up the burning fire inside her blood. He licked at her cream as if it were the tastiest dessert in the world. She zeroed in on his dark head while he imparted pleasure between her thighs.

Whimpers and moans worked up her throat. Breathless, she threw her head back when a spiraling tension gathered inside her. She writhed and groaned. He slipped his tongue into her slick channel and fucked her with quick, merciless swipes.

"Ry... Yes, yes, yes!" She gripped the comforter tight until she held the fabric in a white-knuckle grip.

Need wound into a tight ball inside her. He growled. She knew she'd fall off the edge at any moment. He sucked on her swollen clit, hard. She screamed. Pleasure blasted through her in a tidal wave of shudders. She gasped, trying to catch her breath. He slid his hot body up hers, stopping when the head of his cock kissed her swollen sex.

"I need you."

She twined her hands into his hair and pulled him down for a kiss. They kissed, almost devouring each other with the depth of their lust. She curled her legs around his muscled ass and whimpered. The hard length of his shaft lay between her legs, slipping and sliding over her wet pussy lips. She wanted his hard cock inside.

He pulled his hips back and slid his length into her completely. Her pussy fluttered, grasping at his driving shaft. She moaned at the delicious friction.

"Oh my god."

"You're so tight. God you feel good, but just hold on a second," he said through gritted teeth.

Something wild and untamed inside her took hold. She dug her nails into his shoulders and wiggled her hips under him. She kissed his neck, grazing her teeth over his pounding pulse, and bit his shoulder. He tasted so good. She hauled him further into her pussy by linking her feet together behind his back.

She continued to bite him, and he groaned. "I—I can't hold on…"

"Then don't. Just…fuck me…already."

He slammed into her repeatedly. She whimpered with every drive of his cock into her. Over and over, he thrust and pulled back. She panted and held on for the ride. He groaned, and she moaned with every slap of skin on skin.

"Yes. Just like that. Hard, fast. I love it." Pleasure blasted through her and traveled through her blood in a fiery rush.

His moves became wilder, his thrusts

harsher, faster. With every slide of his cock into her, she saw stars.

"Jesus..." His voice sounded strained.

She lifted off the pillows onto her elbows, swiping her tongue over his shoulder and licking the salty flesh. His taste calmed a hunger she never knew existed inside her. She inhaled deeply, taking in the man, the animal, the instinct to be his. She dropped back onto the pillows. He slipped a hand between their slick bodies and rubbed a finger on her clit.

A swell of intense pleasure rocked her, and air froze in her lungs. She choked out his name as her body shook under him, her pussy gripping his driving cock. He slowed his thrusts and tensed above her. He dropped his head into her shoulder, growled, and licked at her galloping pulse. His cock jerked inside her, spreading warmth into her and filling her womb with his seed.

She took short gulps of air and tried to get her brain to function, but all her nerve endings were still humming in happiness over what just happened. He landed on the bed beside her and quickly moved her to lie in his arms next to him. Exhaustion she'd been feeling since waking claimed her. She shut her eyes and couldn't stop the grin splitting her lips. He'd made her body turn to jelly.

FIFTEEN

Sam woke starving. It had to be pretty late in the day for her to get those types of hunger pangs. Outside the window, the sun was disappearing into the horizon. Eyeing one of Riel's T-shirts, she threw it on for modesty. The shirt landed mid-thigh and was long enough to cover her girly bits. Who knew if he had company below?

Her hair had fallen out of the ponytail she'd had earlier. She pulled the heavy curls into a knot on top of her head. The urge to see Ry and be near him pushed her to move faster.

Quietly making her way down the stairs, she noticed the large bay windows facing the street. Didn't the man believe in curtains? Whoever went by would know what was going on inside the house.

He stood by the stove wearing only a pair of boxers. He had her phone in his hands, tapping on the screen. He gave a nod and set it on the counter, then removed vegetables from a wok and placed them on two plates next to two large steaks. Yum. He must have psychic powers because a steak sounded like exactly what she needed. What she wanted, well, that was another story.

His gaze jerked toward her and heat bloomed on her cheeks. Screw it. It didn't matter that they'd had some amazing sex earlier. She wanted him again. Her body burned for him, and holding back was a struggle, but she managed, if barely. He eyed the T-shirt with so much lust, her temperature zoomed to scorching. Her nipples pebbled, and moisture dripped from her slit.

He sniffed and groaned. "Fuck, Sam. You smell delicious. My appetite has shifted to wanting a taste of honey."

She had no idea what that meant, but she knew no one else smelled as good as he did. Energized and horny, she rushed over to him and wrapped her arms around his neck. Fuck waiting.

His gaze roamed over her face. He was so tall. She had to tilt her head back to look up at him. Well over six feet, he made her feel tiny. She raked her nails into his hair and pulled him down to her. Their lips met, and fireworks went off in her blood. She rubbed her body over his. Whimpers worked from the back of her throat.

He hauled her up by her waist, seating her on the island. Her bare ass rubbed on the cool surface of the counter. The T-shirt came off with a quick rip and tear. With her eyes still shut, she let his scent drift into her nose and burrow deeply into her heart.

The musky, wild animal scent called to an area inside her, a wild, untamed side she never knew existed. He fluttered kisses over her chest and sucked a nipple into his mouth. Molten lava spread through her. She wandered her hands over his muscled chest. She slid a hand down his body, dipped into his boxers, and wrapped it around his cock.

He was hard, hot, and smooth. She pumped his length in a slow glide. He growled, and she smiled, brushing the pad of her thumb over his nipple and pinching the tight little bud.

He sucked on one of her breasts, then the other, and back until she was ready to beg for him to fuck her.

"If I don't have you soon, I may lose the little sanity I have left. I need you." His sexy rumble turned up the heat inside her.

"Then have me. I'm all yours."

His growl only added to the desperation

riding her. He tore off his boxers in the time it took her to let out a soft moan. When he pulled her to the edge of the counter, she thought she'd fall, but he slid her over his cock and slipped inside her in one smooth glide.

She twined her legs and arms around his waist and neck, ending up wrapped tightly around him. Arousal surrounded them like a thick blanket. She smashed her lips to his and moaned into the eager union. He turned, and her back hit the smooth surface of the fridge.

He fucked her mouth with his tongue, mimicking the movements he made with his cock. The fridge moved with each of his thrusts, the contents crashing into each other, making large breaking noises.

Heat spread inside her as he squeezed her ass. The combination of actions made her pussy flutter in seconds. His fast, pummeling drives pushed her to dig her nails into his shoulders. She wrenched her lips from his and moaned louder. Electricity buzzed in her veins, building up the need for more.

"Oh god. Oh yes. Yes, yes, yes." Tight pressure rippled inside her body. Muscles she'd never used before became stiff as she closed the distance to ecstasy. She snapped. A scream lodged in her throat as she came. Pleasure flared brightly, overflowing and rushing through her.

He continued to thrust in and out of her, his nibbles on her jaw and shoulder pushing her orgasm to go on and on. It was moments later that he shuddered. He snarled a curse into her neck and made her body vibrate with the force of his release. Semen shot into her channel and bathed her womb with his cum.

They both panted. He curled a hand around her face and kissed her with so much tenderness, her eyes filled with tears. Dios. She was turning into an emotional ninny.

If she believed in fate, she'd say he was the man for her. But she knew her hormones were probably a little crazy and that's why she wanted him more than any other man in her life.

Shit, the way she was feeling, she was ready to go at it again, and he had just pulled out of her. She'd never been this desperate. It was incredible and scary.

SIXTEEN

They finally sat down to eat and talk. She cut up her food and asked him a question she'd always had. "What does it feel like?"

"What?" He took a bite of steak.

She worried her question might sound intrusive, but she asked it anyway. "To be able to turn into a wolf."

He shrugged. "It's always been a part of me, so it's normal. I'm not sure what I can tell you."

"Come on, you must have more to say than that. All my life, you've been the guys everyone knew not to get into a fight with."

He chuckled. "Believe me, we still get into fights with humans and Other alike."

"Other?"

Their conversation flowed smoothly

through dinner. "Other supernaturals like shifters, demons, witches, warlocks...Other."

"Yeah, Ginny always mentioned Others, but she never spoke much about different shifter types. Is it painful to shift into a werewolf?"

He chewed and frowned, as if trying to figure it out. "Not really. Well, not for born shifters. We are used to shifting from youth, so it's never anything painful. The first time it feels more like an exciting new way to look at the world. Your senses are expanded, you have more strength, and you can fight."

"Is it true that your natural instinct is to kill when shifted into your animal?" With so many of her family members against shifters, she'd always wondered if what they'd said was true.

He glanced up from the plate. "Our first instinct is to protect. If that means we need to kill someone who is hurting or trying to hurt a defenseless person or a loved one, then that's what happens. We have gotten into fights with humans before, and they don't always end up—dead."

She nodded, pleased with his answer, and sipped her iced tea. "I'm kind of jealous of you guys. All of you have these badass animals inside, and I am just a human."

Riel laughed as if she were being silly.

"You're not just human, you're special. What you don't seem to understand is that my wolf is yours to command. Your protection is a priority for him and me."

She wrinkled her nose in confusion. "I'm not sure what that means."

He gave her another one of those hot looks that melted her from the inside and made her forget everything. "It means no one is more important to me than you. I'd give up anything to keep you safe and happy."

That was different. "Happy in the sack?"

"I'd give you all the orgasms in the world to ensure you're sexually fulfilled. But that's not what I meant. I would slay dragons for you."

She swallowed the knot in her throat. As much as she wanted to tell him the same, she knew it was way too soon.

After they ate, Sam decided to head home for a shower. Riel made her promise to return when she was done.

She neared the back door and noticed a package sitting on the step. She pursed her lips and stopped a few yards from the door. She'd been at Riel's house for hours.

Curling her hands into fists, she took a couple of slow steps toward the box. Not expecting anything in the mail made her wary.

She took another step and heard ringing inside the box. She twisted away just as an explosion rocked the back door. A car taking off sounded in the distance.

Propelled by the driving wind of the blast, she landed a few yards away with the backyard awning on top of her.

Dizzy and in pain, she tried to move, but the heavy metal pinned her to the ground. Flames ate the plastic sides of the metal awning and crawled toward her. She was going to kill the asshole that did this. She was ready to scream bloody murder over the flames traveling in her direction. A loud growl stopped her in place.

Stunned, she glanced to her left. Riel rushed toward her. He grabbed the metal and flung it off her with the flick of a wrist. Troy joined him a moment later.

Troy used a fire extinguisher to fight the flames eating the back door of her house. She groaned and winced with each slight move. The ponytail she'd donned after leaving Riel's house hung in a mess to her side. Riel picked her up in his arms and carried her across his yard to lay her on a lounger.

"Are you okay? Tell me what hurts." His gaze roamed her face and body.

She moved her arms and legs, searching for

injuries. "My shoulder hurts like hell and so does my thigh, but other than that, I'm fine, I think."

"Your face is bleeding." He touched her chin with the tip of a finger. "Stay here. I'm going to help Troy, and then I'll check out your shoulder."

The fire tried to spread over the back of her house. Troy used an extinguisher to fight the bright heat. A few moments later, Riel joined him with his water hose. The water quickly doused the flames, and the charred door fell off the hinges. She fixed her hair and sighed in happiness that they'd been able to stop the fire from spreading into the house. Both men turned toward her. Riel headed into his house while Troy sat in a chair near her.

Troy's frown was fierce. "Someone is trying to hurt you, Sam."

The words turned her blood to ice. Could one of her relatives really stoop that low? She almost snorted. What kind of stupid question was that? Claro. Of course, they would. If they killed her, they'd be able to split the money amongst themselves. No need to worry about Sam. It made sense to try to get her out of the way.

Riel marched out with a first aid kit. He sat next to her and pulled out gauze and alcohol pads. While he cleaned her chin, she wondered about Juan Junior. He hated her enough to shoot her, of that she had no doubt. She just hadn't thought he'd go this far.

"Sam, we need to know more about your relatives," Troy said while Riel swiped the alcohol pad over her shoulder.

The bruise hurt, but she was too shocked that someone had actually tried to kill her to feel much of the pain.

Riel shook his head. "First, I need to take her to the clinic. I need to make sure she doesn't have any other injuries."

"But I feel fine." He scowled at her. "Okay, other than my shoulder, I don't feel like anything's broken."

He cupped her jaw. "I'm not taking any chances. You could have internal bleeding. You can agree or disagree, but we're going." His tone left no room for argument.

"I'll come with you guys. I'll drive, and you both sit in the back," Troy headed to the navy SUV.

Riel picked her up and carried her to the vehicle. Once they reached the clinic, the pack doctor set her on a bed. After the doctor introduced herself as Raven, she looked Sam over. The doctor was young.

"We're going to do a CT scan, an MRI, and we're going to take some blood just to be sure all is as it should be, okay, Samira?" Raven smiled and patted her hand.

"That's fine. Thanks, and please, call me Sam."

"Don't worry, Sam. Nothing we do will add to your discomfort."

Raven was short like Sam. Knowing shifters tended to be taller, Sam asked the question burning on her tongue. "Are you a shifter, too?"

The doctor placed a stethoscope to Sam's chest and listened. "No. I'm just a human."

Raven also had the most amazing amethyst-colored eyes. If they were contacts, they looked great on the doctor.

"Me too."

"Let's get you some tests now, okay?"

She nodded and allowed them to do the multitude of tests without argument. She wanted to pacify Riel and let him see she was fine. Why that was important, she didn't know. All she knew was that he'd been so considerate with her, she wanted him to stop worrying over the minor injuries she'd suffered.

The doctor gave her strong painkillers for the bruises on her body. Unfortunately, her shoulder hadn't been the only area hurt in the explosion. Raven had discovered other, bigger bruises.

They left after a few hours with Troy acting

as chauffeur again. The heavy painkillers had started to take effect. She lay on Riel's lap, relaxed to the point where she wanted to just lie in his arms forever.

She snuggled into him and sniffed his neck. "You smell good," she murmured softly.

"I do?" He sounded shocked.

She flicked her tongue over his throat. "Mmm-hmm. Delicious. Like nature, earth, and something else that's driving me crazy. It makes me want to strip you down and eat you."

SEVENTEEN

Riel's heart pounded hard while Sam slept in his arms. She'd fallen asleep just seconds after telling him how good he smelled. It made him wonder at her shifter status again.

Wolf shifters had a very keen sense of smell. When in heat, their mate scented better than anyone else to them. He'd called Sophia while Sam had been getting her scan and asked if she would check out Sam's blood in her lab.

She'd promised to call Raven to get a sample so she could look into Sam's DNA. Something about the way she acted screamed shifter, but she didn't have the scent of an animal. It confused the hell out of him.

When he placed her on his bed, her brow furrowed, and she moaned in pain. Anger surged through him. It was clear someone was after his mate. What he didn't know was why.

Too many things had been going on at the same time. Not to mention, he needed to speak to her about their bond. The animal inside him recognized her as his. Nothing would change that, and he needed to figure out a way to make her understand. His gut clenched. For someone to get to Sam, they would have to go through him first.

* * *

"All right. I'll let him know." Troy shut off the phone as Riel walked into the kitchen.

"What's going on?"

"That was Chase. He said to let you know he can send others to help if you feel you need backup here. I told him to hold off for now. He also said Sophia has the blood sample and will get back to you as soon as she can figure out anything of importance. But it may take a few days because she's exhausted and needs tons of sleep."

Riel sighed and sat at the kitchen table. "I know. Did you question the teens in the area today?"

Troy nodded, grabbed his soda can and sat in a chair across from Riel. "Yeah. I got around to the families in the vicinity, but none of them were in the area at the time of the bombing."

Riel scratched his beard stubble. What was really bothering him was Sam's reaction to smelling him.

She'd acted just as a female of his kind when in heat earlier. Her sweet scent still invaded his senses. There was just something different about it. It was faint, but she still had the wild look when he'd been inside her, as if a small, untamed part of her wanted out of an invisible cage. "I need you to do me another favor."

Troy jerked his head in a nod. "Anything you need, bro."

"Can you check out her family history? I want to know if there are any shifters in her background."

Troy lifted his brows in surprise. "I did get the faint scent of something from her. Not strong enough to call animal, but there's something there. Is that what's got you wondering?"

Riel massaged a hand over the back of his neck. "Yes, but also her actions. They are so similar to those of a female in heat. It's weird. It could also be she was bitten by a werewolf while in the jungle and just wasn't aware."

Troy shook his head and drank from his can. "I don't think so. If she was bitten, she'd have had her change by now."

"What if something in her genetic makeup didn't allow her to fully shift? Maybe an anomaly?" He growled in frustration. "I don't know. It just doesn't feel right. She's not what she thinks. I can tell because just her scent is driving me into needing to mate her whenever I'm near her. This is more... This is different. I have to figure it out before something else happens."

"Have you considered that maybe she's just a human with some extra hormones that make her susceptible to our kind?"

If that were true, then she might not want him personally but as a boy toy. Maybe her hormones were pushing her to have sex with him to sate her own need to breed.

He didn't want Sam to be with him because of some physical need to have sex in general; he wanted her to want him, to want to be with him, to love him. Fuck. He knew he'd lost his heart to her the first time he'd looked into her big brown eyes. She'd just returned home from boarding school and was about to head off to college.

Happiness had filled his soul when she'd smiled at him for the very first time. At that moment, he knew she was the only woman for him.

He didn't believe for a second she was hormonal or desperate to breed. Someone knocked on his door before he had a chance to say that. Seconds later, footsteps headed toward the kitchen. Nat and Kane walked in together. Troy growled, and Riel sighed.

Nat pursed her lips. "Put a sock in it, Casanova. Where's Sam? We came as soon as we heard."

"She's sleeping." Riel glanced back and forth between Kane and Troy. It was his deepest hope they wouldn't wake Sam because then he'd have to kick both their asses.

Nat folded her arms over her chest. "So, what happened?"

"Small homemade bomb. She mentioned she heard ringing coming from inside the box right before it detonated and a car taking off right after the explosion. It was enough to cause some serious damage, possibly death, if she'd been holding it."

Nat covered her mouth with her hand, wide-eyed.

He knew what she was thinking. What if Sam had been holding the box? He needed to figure this out now. He wouldn't rest until he knew she wasn't under any kind of threat. Nat knew Sam better than anyone else. They could question her and cross things off their need-to-know list.

He motioned toward the chairs. "Tell me

about her family. I know they're a bunch of lowlifes, but we need more detail than that."

Nat sat across from him and made a point to ignore Troy's glare. Riel wanted to remind his friend that this wasn't the time for a lovers' quarrel. He had a feeling Kane wasn't sleeping with Nat. If he had a guess, she was using Kane to piss off Troy, but the green-eyed monster of jealousy didn't let the normally levelheaded Troy see it.

She placed her elbow on the table and cupped her cheek with a hand. "Well, there's Ginny, who we all knew. She was the matriarch and the sweetest woman in the world. She was also very concerned for Sam. She always said she needed to keep her away from the rest of the vultures so she'd never end up hurt. But I think she underestimated their greed when she left the money in Sam's name."

"What do you mean hurt?" Kane asked.

"I think it was more of an emotional thing. Sam's mom was kind of a spirit. She loved hanging with shifters and never cared what her family thought. It was frowned upon for the youngest daughter to be hanging with the 'animals,' as they liked to say."

Riel clenched his jaw. Figured, there were always those that knew of his kind and thought of them as just a bunch of beasts.

Nat's voice continued to fill the kitchen space. "Then we have the aunts, Margarita — Maggie — Cecilia, and Luisa. I'm not sure what Margarita or Cecilia have been up to, but those two are the worst evil bitches you'd ever heard of. The wicked witch has nothing on them.

"Sam kind of felt bad for Luisa. According to Sam, Luisa let her sisters and brother pressure her into agreeing with them.

"Then there's Juan, the brother. He's never around since he's always chasing a skirt halfway around the world. I think he's living in the Philippines right now. He's got his own inheritance from his father's side, so he never cared about this side of his family.

"Apparently his father is old school and planned on leaving all his money to his only son. But now, his father isn't sharing his inheritance with Junior, so he's dependent on whatever Ginny left him. He's one to watch out for."

Kane got up and grabbed two sodas from the fridge. He brought a glass with ice for Nat and sat down.

His two friends stared each other down. Troy snarled at Kane, but then focused on Nat. "Why is Juan Junior someone to watch?"

Nat popped the can, filled the sweaty glass, and took a sip. "He's an avid shooter and likes to intimidate people with his guns. In fact, Sam mentioned how he acted as if he wanted to drag her out back and put a couple of slugs in her for being the sole inheritor."

EIGHTEEN

Riel's gut clenched. He didn't like the sound of that. Any person that carried a weapon and had an attitude problem was already a risk. When you added that he felt cheated over a multi-billion-dollar inheritance, there was more than a good possibility he might have something to do with wanting to get Sam out of the way.

Troy jumped in again. "Are there any other relatives we need to know about?"

Nat furrowed her brow. "Hmm. Cecilia has no kids and neither does Maggie, although Maggie's husband has been said to have ties to the mob. He's a dangerous one too.

"Luisa's kids, from what I've heard, travel and have successful careers, so I don't think they're interested in anything. The only other person is Marcia, Juan Junior's wife."

She shook her head and sighed. "She isn't a threat, more like a victim. Sam thinks he beats on her, but she refuses to leave him. It's one of those situations where she'll put up with anything just to have a nice house and expensive things."

Disgust rolled through Riel. What a piece-of-shit excuse for a man. He curled his hands into fists, and a low growl worked up his throat. It bothered him that a man would hurt a woman, especially his mate. His father had always told him that mates were a rare treasure and should be cared for and protected at all costs. How could any man in good conscience hurt the woman they claimed to love?

The sound of gunshots exploded outside. Troy pulled Nat to the ground and threw himself over her.

Instinct took over, and Riel shifted into his wolf. His clothes tore at the seams, and he ran for the door. When he reached the front, he realized the gunshots hadn't been toward his home. He ran in the direction of the scent of gunpowder and ended up in front of Sam's house. Broken glass littered the ground, and the smell of whiskey and tobacco lingered.

A black wolf ran up to him. Kane.

Kane sniffed the ground around the front of

the house. "Did you see anyone?"

"No. I think they must've been shooting as they drove. When I got out here, there wasn't a car in sight, but I still smell whiskey and tobacco." Riel continued to smell the same spot he figured was where the car slowed to shoot.

Kane snarled. "I do as well. I also smell sweat and something else."

A low growl came out of Riel. "Sweet." Whoever was after Sam had a woman with them.

Kane growled. "Yes."

Riel glanced back at the broken windows. At this rate, she'd end up homeless in a week, the way her house kept getting attacked. He'd call in others to help fix the back door and her windows in the morning. "It's the same scent we got from the bomb in the yard."

Kane sniffed and turned toward Riel's home. "Someone really wants to get at Sam."

Riel followed behind slowly. He wouldn't let anyone get to her. She was his, and he'd be damned if now that he finally had a chance to be with her, some asshole would hurt her. Not in his fucking lifetime.

Riel and Kane went back to the house. Being a shifter and never knowing when he'd need to change, he kept a closet full of clothes everywhere, including his car. He and Kane dressed and went into the kitchen. Troy was the only person in there.

Kane frowned at Troy. "Where's Nat?"

"She went up to check on Sam. She didn't want her to wake up scared if the noise got through her drug-induced sleep." Troy stood and faced Riel. "I'll look into Juan Junior."

Riel wanted a piece of the man himself, but he didn't want to leave Sam alone.

Kane nodded. "And I'll find out more about the others."

As they all headed to the front, Nat came down the stairs. "She's still fast asleep. I am pretty sure she's going to go all night like this." She fixed her gaze on Riel. "Take care of her. She's been through hell the past few weeks, and I'd hate to see her hurt any further."

If it were up to Riel, Sam would never even get a headache for the rest of her life. He nodded and the three left his house.

When he got back upstairs, he showered and lay next to Sam on the bed. She turned to face him, snuggled into his side, and sighed his name. Satisfaction filled his heart.

Riel woke to the sound of his phone buzzing on the bedside table. He was about to reach for it when another hand curled over his hand and placed it over a naked breast. He snapped his eyes open. What he saw took his breath away.

Sam straddled his hips, her long curls hanging in a dark, silky curtain down to her elbows. The brown of her eyes was bright and clear from the long sleep. She had a sexy smirk on her face and was, much to his delight, completely naked. He mentally devoured the curve of her shoulders, her perfectly full breasts with berry-tipped nipples, the sexy indent of her waist, and down to her gleaming hot sex resting over his stiff cock.

"How are you feeling?" Maybe they should hold off on sex until she felt better. Not that his dick gave a crap about his concern. He was harder than a piece of steel and desperately wanted inside her wet heat.

She grinned, lowered her head, and licked one of his nipples. "Like I want you to fuck me until my brain turns to mush, my toes curl, and you make me come." His blood rushed down to his cock.

He groaned. "If I'm dreaming don't wake me up, unless I'm humping the pillow. I'd hate for you to see me doing that."

She laughed and wiggled over him. He didn't think it possible, but his cock grew more and jerked. He lay there, enthralled with her movements. She twirled her tongue over one flat disc and then wrapped her lips around the tiny bud and sucked.

His hips rocked under her, and his cock slid between her pussy lips, covering his erection with her dripping honey.

Desire shot through his body and deepened his voice to a low growl. "I want you so badly, I can't think straight."

She licked her way down his abs and dipped her tongue into his belly button. "Then don't think, my big, sexy wolf, just feel." Her whisper was so low that if he didn't have enhanced hearing, he wouldn't have picked up on her term of endearment. Possession roared to life inside him. She'd called him hers. She slid down his body until her breath kissed his jutting cock.

Fisting the sheets under him, he panted. She wrapped a small hand around his dick, licking a slow trail from root to tip. He groaned and tore at the sheets. The sound of ripping material was loud in the room, but he couldn't look away from the sexiest sight in the world.

One second Sam was flicking her tongue around the crown of his cock, and the next she had shoved half of it into her mouth. Holy fuck. Wet suction tightened around his shaft until all he knew was the hot slide of her lips over him.

"Goddamn, Sam. You're incredible." He panted and fisted more of the sheets to keep from shoving himself down her throat.

When her hair got in the way of his view, he released the sheets and roped the long mass in his grip. She was amazing. He wanted to thank god for her lips…and her tongue. He thrust into her mouth, and she continued to bob her head over his shiny cock. She jerked at the base of his shaft, driving the fire in his blood to a boiling point.

Goddamn! She started humming around his dick, causing a new vibration, and he snapped. He curled his hands on her arms and pulled her up. Her sexy smirk told him she knew how close to the edge he was. He grunted when she gripped his cock and slid down until he was impaling her completely. His breath hissed out of his lungs as she moaned and threw her head back. The move shoved her breasts out in a silent offering, one he wasn't going to ignore. He clutched her hips and helped her ride him.

Rising off the bed, he lifted his head, sucking a bouncing nipple into his mouth. She whimpered and moaned loudly. The sound drove the hunger inside him. It was a difficult task to rein in the beast so he could treat her gently. She dug her nails into his shoulders until he smelled blood. That he made her lose control added to the arousal coursing through him.

Her taste consumed him. He sucked her nipple deeply into his mouth and bit down on the hard little bud. She jerked above him, and her pussy walls fluttered around his cock. He did it again to the other one. His little mate liked it when he bit. And by god, he loved it, too.

"Oh, yes, yes, yes." Her whimpers were loud, desperate.

Riel let go of her nipple and leaned back into the pillows. He gripped her hips and increased the pace of lifting and dropping her over his cock. The scent of sex, wild and untamed, filled the room. She panted his name in husky groans, each call for him making him feel invincible.

"Ry, Ry, Ry... Please," she begged, digging her nails into his abs.

Her face was flushed, lust riding her high. "What do you want, sweetheart?"

She glanced at him with so much need, he knew he'd do anything for her. Her eyes were glazed with desire. "Make me come. Please."

He moved a hand between her slick pussy lips and rubbed a thumb over her peeking clit. Her breath hitched, and she tensed above him. Her movements became jerky and uncoordinated. Tweaking the sensitive nerve bundle between two fingers, he watched her soar.

"Oh...yes!" She choked out a scream.

Her pussy gripped at his shaft and sucked him in. Panting, he clenched his jaw. With deep breaths, he continued to lift and impale her on his cock, her pussy gripping him in a silken hold. He had to fight her tightened vaginal walls to get in and out of her sex.

His orgasm hit him square in the chest, blindsiding him. He groaned as electric pleasure traveled down his spine. A loud snarl tore from him. He ground his dick into her pussy and came into her channel for long moments, the sound of their loud breathing the only noise heard.

Sam ended up draped over his chest, her face in the crook of his neck. She licked at the beads of sweat that ran down his throat. He got up from the bed and set up the shower, then returned and lifted her into his arms.

She immediately wrapped her legs around his waist. "What are you doing? I weigh a ton, and you keep lifting me like I weigh nothing."

He chuckled through the kisses she rained over his face. "You forget I have more strength than a human man, and you're not as heavy as you think."

"Mm…yes, I am. Where are we going?" she whispered, nibbling on his earlobe.

She was unbelievable. It was a good thing all he wanted to do was slide into her whenever she was around, because she was insatiable. "We're going to take a shower." He sighed in contentment when she giggled.

NINETEEN

After an incredible, admittedly long, shower they went back to his bedroom. Sam still felt ready to have another round of the sexy werewolf. She didn't know why but thinking of him all wild and untamed lit a slow fire in her blood.

It pushed her to get him in her body again. If she didn't know better, she'd swear she was turning into some kind of cat in heat. Her sole focus had become Riel and getting him to stroke her insides with his cock. She shuddered, remembering how good he felt driving in and out of her.

Had it not been so damn pleasurable, she'd be worried. Her pussy clenched at the thought of having him again, filling her with his seed and marking her. Wait, what? Since when did she care about markings?

A fuzzy feeling entered her heart. He'd been taking care of her and had been so concerned, she couldn't help but wonder if something long-term could grow between them.

Great sex was one thing, but that wasn't her priority in life anymore. She wanted a man to love her and want her whether she was young and perky or old and fat…and finding a man like that was like looking for a needle in a haystack.

Riel had been so caring and thoughtful in the past three days, she didn't know what to think. Her brain told her it was too soon to have feelings, but her heart screamed at her to grab him and never let go. What the hell was she supposed to do?

She dressed in the previous day's clothes. Riel picked up his cell phone, frowning as he listened to his messages. The heat in his eyes was enough to have her pussy dripping again. She was in deep shit. All the man had to do was look at her and she was panting and ready to get on all fours.

He pressed a button and moved the phone to his ear. "Sophia, you called me? Now? Yes. No, we'll come to you." He hung up. "We need to go see Sophia. She wants to talk to you about your blood."

Was she sick? Did something come up she didn't know about? She looked into Riel's eyes and knew that no matter what Sophia said, everything would work itself out.

When they arrived at Sophia and Chase's house, Sam was greeted by a really tall man holding Selena. The alpha, Chase Blackburn. He was a few inches taller than Ry and much more muscular, yet the only impression she got was of a concerned husband. He was fawning over the petite brunette she'd come to see, Sophia.

Sophia jiggled Shane in her arms. The little boy lifted his arms to Sam the moment he noticed her.

"My Sam," Shane's little voice called.

Sam's heart melted. "Seriously, can I adopt him off you? I promise to treat him right, overfeed him, and never let him out of my arms. I'm in love with this boy. He's so precious, and those chubby cheeks just drive me crazy."

Everyone laughed when Shane attached his mouth to Sam's cheek and tried to bite her.

Sophia giggled and tickled her son on the side. "Uh-oh, Shane. I think Uncle Ry might have a problem with anyone else biting on his mate."

Sam lifted her brows. Ry's mate? What was she talking about? She turned to Ry. He gave her a look that dared her to say anything against that. Like she knew what the hell that meant.

Chase motioned for Riel to take Shane and

turned to Sam. "We'll take the kids, and you can go into Sophia's lab and talk."

Sam let go of Shane with a pout and followed Sophia down a hallway, through a set of secured doors and into a cold lab.

"Wow. I can't believe you have this in your house."

Sophia grinned and sat at a desk. Her hair was up in a messy bun, and her T-shirt had handprint marks on the front with the names of her kids under each print.

"It was either have my own lab at home or Chase was going to have to put up with me working long hours away from home.

"He prefers for me to do anything that's not related to my cancer research here. It's safer for the pack. I tend to go overboard when I work. They're scared I'll do something weird and turn everyone into a different animal if I'm not supervised."

She rolled her eyes. "Seriously, though, like there's anything out there that's cooler than a werewolf? I mean a unicorn would be awesome, but I haven't run into any of those." She smiled.

Sam laughed and took the seat across from Sophia's desk. "So can you tell me what it is about my blood that caught your attention?"

Sophia flicked through papers before

stopping and focusing her attention on Sam. "The reason I asked you if you were shifter is because there's a partial code in your DNA for the shifter chromosome."

What was she saying? "I'm sorry. I don't understand what you mean."

Sophia smiled apologetically. "Sorry, I tend to forget not everyone speaks geek. Okay. Think of it this way: your mom gave you some of her genes, and your dad gave you some of his. They blend together and make up Sam.

"Normally that means you'll either be a shifter or a human. However, in your case, I've found that you have a partial link. Almost as if you were meant to be a shifter but somehow the other leg necessary to make up the full gene was removed."

Sam laughed, thinking Sophia was kidding. "So, you're saying you think I have a werewolf inside?"

Sophia shook her head, glanced down at the papers on her desk and then back at Sam, her lips no longer curled up in laughter. "Not really. What you have are some of the traits since you don't have an animal. Trust me, I checked."

Sam really thought there might be a mistake with her blood work. There was no way she could have any shifter traits inside. "I think you might be mistaken."

Sophia bit her lip. "Have you encountered anything different lately? Enhanced sense of smell? Sight? Arousal? Sorry to get so personal, but it's important." She lifted her brows and waited.

The beating of her heart made it almost impossible to hear Sophia's questions. Since she'd been bitten in Brazil, she'd been seeing things at a farther distance with more clarity, even in the dark. And her sense of smell had gotten incredibly acute. But what made her palms sweat was the arousal bit.

For the past three days, she'd been desperate in her need to have sex with Riel. She'd brushed it off as having been ignorant of her needs for too long, but now she wasn't so sure. A cement block settled in her stomach. "What does that mean?"

Sophia's brow puckered. "Which part?"

TWENTY

Sam gulped. "All of it. Especially the sex part. What if I...I've had better sight and smell. What if I'm hornier than a bunny and can't get enough sex to save my life?" Her voice rose to a hysterical pitch.

Sophia gave her hand a gentle squeeze. "Calm down, Sam. I know how you feel. But what you have to realize is this has always been you. When you were bitten in the jungle, the animal that bit you was a werewolf.

"He couldn't turn you because you already had the partial gene in your cells. That means the bite only served to awaken dormant traits. You can't turn into an animal because the gene is not complete, but you have some of the traits. And one is the mating heat. Right now, you are in full-blown heat."

She stared wide-eyed at Sophia. "So, this desperate need for sex, will it go away?"

Sophia lifted one brow. "Do you want it to?"

Did she want it to? Of course! She wasn't an animal. She shouldn't be in heat! But wait, if the heat went away, did that mean she'd stop wanting Riel? "If it goes away, will I still want to have sex?"

Sophia laughed, her eyes twinkling. "That's one thing you don't have to worry about. The difference between regular sex and in-heat sex is that when in heat, all your body wants is for your mate to breed with you until you're pregnant. The hunger doesn't go away until you're either pregnant or see the full heat through. It's the way our species survives and thrives."

Sam's mind whirled a million miles per hour.

Hold on just a second. Did she say mate and pregnant in the same sentence? "What exactly do you mean mate? I don't have a mate."

"I think you do. And I think you know it, too."

Sam knew she was right. Ry. She'd had feelings for the man since the first time she'd laid eyes on him when she was eighteen. The invisible link had always scared her, but now that they'd been together, she couldn't imagine being apart from him.

"But don't you need to go through some kind of ritual to be someone's mate?" She'd heard something but wasn't sure what that meant.

Sophia's eyes softened. "Well...it's more of what he does that seals the bond."

Sam wanted to jump over the desk and shake the other woman. Sophia was having too much fun at her expense and taking too damn long to explain. "What does he have to do?"

Sophia giggled and sighed, her voice turning wistful. "He bites the back of your shoulder and fills your womb with his...er...semen."

Did that mean— "But Riel already came inside me. We've been having sex like rabbits. So does that mean I can be pregnant?"

Sophia sniffed. "I'm not scenting any changes in your hormone levels. Has he bitten you?"

Sam ran a hand through her hair and made her ponytail fall. "He's given me a few love bites, but what does that have to do with anything?" She fixed her hair and wondered if she was nuts or if Sophia was the crazy one. Somehow, she doubted Sophia, renowned geneticist, would screw with her just for kicks.

"I'm not sure how this works, but trust me, I'm looking into it. I think a male can only get his mate pregnant after he's given her the mate bite. A mate bite isn't a little love bite.

"He'll have to bite down hard on the back of your shoulder, embedding his canines into your skin and drawing blood. By doing that, he'll be able to mix his saliva with your blood and give you a new scent. You'll scent of him.

"All other shifters will know you're his mate. I'm not sure if you can get pregnant before mating, but I do know your heat won't end unless you get pregnant or get through your heat.

"So you can't be pregnant. If his seed had taken inside you, you wouldn't be feeling horny as hell anymore." Sophia tapped a short pink nail to her chin.

So if she was Ry's mate, why hadn't he bitten her?

As if she had read her mind, Sophia answered her. "I think he's giving you the choice. Ry is one of the most thoughtful men I know. He would never take away your right to choose. This isn't marriage. This is a much deeper connection. It's soul bonding. If you want to be his mate, you're going to have to tell him to bite you."

Sam was even more confused now. She ran her sweaty palms over her shorts. "But if it's that deep and committed, how do I know that's what he wants? What if he hasn't done it because he just doesn't want to?"

Sophia shrugged and gave her a small smile. "I can't tell you what to do. I can only tell you that whatever your heart is telling you is probably right. Our brains tend to overanalyze things until we don't know which way to go. Follow your instinct."

Her instincts told her to stay with Ry. What did her heart say? That she loved the sexy, caring, and hot-as-hell wolf. Just thinking of him made her breath hitch, her heart flip, and a warm, marshmallowy emotion run rampant in her stomach.

The question was did he love her? She couldn't ask him that…could she? Oh, who the fuck was she kidding? If she wanted to have a long-term relationship with him, which she did, she'd have to grab the bull by the horns. She'd have to pretty much tell him to mate with her, or he'd never do it.

He probably thought he would infringe on her rights to decide. The stupid, thoughtful, sexy beast. God, she loved that man. And she was keeping him.

Sophia's voice broke through her thoughts. "Can you do me a favor?"

Sam glanced up. The dilemma of her love life no longer seemed so confusing. "Sure. You've done so much for me today, what do you need?"

Sophia scrunched her nose in thought. "I'd like to find out more about your past and why you're not a full-blown shifter, or it will drive me bananas. Do you have any family records you can rifle through? I would really like some details on your family history to see what has made you the way you are."

Now that she mentioned it, Sam remembered Ginny had a trunk full of old family information. "Yes. That's not a problem. I do have things to go through, so as soon as I find anything of value, I'll bring it over."

Sophia sighed. "Thank you. I've just never seen anything like you before. It's your right to know why you can't shift and, more importantly, how you came to have the shifter traits. Plus, we'll want to know if your future offspring will be able to shift."

Sam nodded. "Thanks. I do want to know." She stood and walked out with Sophia.

They found Chase and Ry in the backyard on their stomachs while the kids played horsey and bounced on the men's backs. Sam grinned and couldn't help laughing when Selena pulled at Riel's hair and giggled. He'd make a great father. Her womb clenched as if in agreement.

It was time to get him back to the house and

have her way with her mate. Shifter or not, he was hers, and they both knew it. The link between them had been tangible since the first time their gazes met.

While he drove them back to the house, her thoughts centered on getting him to admit how he felt for her. If he was waiting for her to make the choice, then she was waiting for him to open his mouth.

When they reached his house, Nat was sitting on one of his front steps and waved at them. He parked and walked both women inside. Just as they entered, his phone rang. Moments later, he pulled Sam off to the side and into his arms.

"I need to go Kane's. He's got information and can't get to me. Don't leave the house. I'll be back shortly, and then we need to talk." He lowered his head and kissed her until all she knew was the firm stroking of his lips and the sexy invasion of his tongue in her mouth.

Once he left, Sam turned to Nat. Her friend grinned from ear to ear. "So...when's the wedding?"

TWENTY-ONE

"You're out of your mind." Sam laughed. "And what are you doing here anyway?" Her heart told her all she needed was for Riel to admit he loved her and bite her, claiming her as his mate. If he happened to ask her to marry him then she'd say yes. What woman didn't want to marry the man she loved? But her main concern was getting her mate to claim her.

Nat said, "I wanted to talk to see if you can remember anything else about your family. Does Ginny have photo albums or written notes about your wonderful fam?"

This was the perfect opportunity for Sam to find the small trunk Ginny kept all the important personal papers in. Maybe she would be able to figure out how the strange shifter link had emerged in her life.

"Let me run over to the house. I have something I need to pick up anyway. Do me a favor and make a sandwich for me. I'm starving. Ry and I ran out without getting a chance to eat."

Nat waggled her brows. "Yeah. I can imagine what kept you so busy you didn't get a chance to eat." She laughed. "Go. I'll have something by the time you get back."

Guilt made her rush. Ry had told her to stay in his house, but she wasn't going to be gone long, and she really wanted to know who the shifter was in her family.

After unlocking the front door, she dropped the key on the coffee table before she ran up to Ginny's room. Once there, she was overcome with sadness. She'd been avoiding Ginny's room, knowing it would be difficult to handle. The soft gold and purple tones decorating the room were Ginny's favorite colors.

Pictures of Sam through the years hung on the walls and sat on every surface in the room. Moisture gathered in her eyes, making her vision blurry.

Grief tore through her, roping around her heart and squeezing hard. She took a breath, and a sob escaped. Tears fell on her cheeks, and she wiped them with the back of her hand. Her heart ached for the woman who'd taught her right from wrong and to be the person she wanted to be.

She'd loved her unconditionally. She'd never hear her grandmother's soft Latin accent telling her to live her life to the fullest. She'd never hug her tiny frame or brush her short, raven bob. But worst of all, she'd never be able to tell her how much she loved her.

She choked on her sobs. Taking choppy breaths, she swallowed at the knot in her throat and sighed. If only she'd been back before Ginny had died, but it was too late to change the past. And Ginny would never have allowed her to. She'd tell her to move on and let go of whatever went wrong, learn from it, and use it to make better decisions in the future.

Steeling her spine, she stepped forward. Ginny had always told her not to cry for her when she died. She'd enjoyed her life and didn't want anyone mourning her.

It had been hard to do as Ginny asked the first few days when pain and loss had filled her heart. Now she had so much going on, she knew what Ginny meant when she told her to live her life the way she wanted to be remembered. All she wanted was to find one man who would love her and who she could love for the rest of her life.

The image of Ry's face filled her mind. She no longer had a doubt he was the right man for her, and she'd tell him as soon as he returned home.

She marched toward the large trunk at the end of Ginny's bed. The latch came open, and she lifted the lid to find the small trunk she needed. Thank goodness Ginny never moved it to a new spot.

Although small, the trunk was heavy and a bit clunky.

As she hurried by the kitchen table, she snatched up the packet containing the will Mr. Carson had given her. This would be a good time to flip through it and see what else the will contained. She also remembered he had asked her to stop by his office. She made a mental note while heading toward the front door.

Since both hands were full, she bypassed the key on the small table and used her foot to pull the door to. It didn't latch but was closed enough for the minute it would take to get back.

Breathless and panting, she ran back to Ry's house. When she got to the kitchen, she collapsed on a chair, placing the trunk on the large kitchen table.

Nat chuckled at Sam's panting and brought her a glass of water. "You okay?"

She nodded and drank the cold liquid and stood slowly, taking her sweet time after having carried the heavy little trunk. "I'll be right back. Gotta lock the front door."

Out the door again, she walked back to her house, Nat's laughter floating from the kitchen. She pushed the door open and went to the coffee table.

A strange smell permeated the air. She frowned and marched into the kitchen to look for the reason behind the fragrance.

As she entered, someone grabbed her from behind. Like manacles, two big arms held her in place while a black material was placed over her head. She screamed and kicked to no avail. The arms around her chest tightened until she struggled to get air into her lungs.

She felt a painful piercing on her arm, which made her wince, followed by a burning sensation, and then the numbing of her arm. Oh god. She'd been injected with something. Whatever they'd given her worked quickly.

Her muscles turned heavy, and her struggles sluggish. Weighed down by her unhelpful arms and legs, her efforts waned even when she tried to fight back. Her screams grew muffled, until they stopped altogether due to her oxygen-deprived lungs.

The arms, which she was sure belonged to a giant, hauled her up steps and a massive body fell on a bed on top of her, pinning her down. The smell of male sweat, cigars, and whiskey told her the person holding her down was a man. He wasn't alone.

While the man's large body robbed her of the oxygen needed to stay alive, someone grabbed her feet. A coarse rope tangled around her legs until she couldn't kick anymore. Her arms were jerked over her head and also bound in a painfully tight grip.

Whatever was holding her arms down was cutting off the circulation in her wrists. She still couldn't get enough air into her lungs with the man's heavy body draped over her.

Every noise became enhanced. She heard the quiet whispers from one to the other. It took great effort to fight the drowsiness taking hold of her.

"That's it." The scratchy whisper sounded like a smoker that had a horribly dry throat.

"You're sure." The second voice wasn't right. It sounded as if the person was trying to sound different on purpose.

"Yes. She can't get out of these binds," the scratchy voice whispered.

"Okay. I'll set the fire and meet you in the back. Let's get the hell out of here."

Shit. They were going to set the house on fire with her inside. She tugged at her arms to no avail. Every pull made her wince. Exhaustion dragged at her, and she blinked inside her head covering.

She shook her head side to side until she was able to see light under the dark cloth. When the scent of smoke reached her, her blood turned to ice. Frantic, she shook her head and shrugged her shoulders until the cloth came off completely.

She could now look around her room. Filling her lungs with air, she let out the loudest scream of her life, hoping someone would hear her.

Panic seized her when she saw flames licking at the door frame to her bedroom. She was going to die. No! It was wrong. There had to be a way to get out.

She tugged at her almost-numb legs and arms, but only chafed her wrists in the process. It took her a moment to realize she was screaming for Riel. Her mind had focused on him, seeking out the one man she knew would do anything to save her, as the room filled with smoke.

With every scream, she inhaled copious amounts of smoke. She coughed and breathed into her shoulder as flames crawled into her room. Horror filled her as all the memories from her childhood were destroyed by the hungry blaze.

Metal frames melted, photos turned to ash, and her lovely blue wood furniture all turned dark with the force of the fire eating its way through her room.

Smoke made her eyes water and her lungs burn. She couldn't get air in. Every time she inhaled, her lungs screamed in agony, and she coughed in pain. The drug attempted to pull her to sleep and forget about breathing.

White spots danced before her eyes, and her vision swam, the lack of oxygen making her lightheaded. A loud growl made her jerk her gaze to the door. A blurry Riel ran into the room, soaking wet.

Determination lined his features, concern visible in his eyes. He moved up to her arms and beat at the wood until the rope came loose. She was still bound and trying to get air in. He picked her up and held her in his arms. The last thing she knew, her body was flying through the air before darkness consumed her.

TWENTY-TWO

Riel dropped Sam's limp body out of the window into Troy's waiting arms. As soon as he caught her, Riel jumped, landing in a crouch. There had been no way he could have gone out the door. The house was consumed in the blazing inferno.

He immediately ran over to Sam. They laid her on the ground, and he felt for a pulse. She wasn't breathing. He started CPR, tilting her head back and blowing air into her lungs. Nothing. His entire life narrowed down to getting her to breathe. If he didn't achieve that, nothing else mattered.

"Breathe, baby." He pumped her chest and blew into her lungs. "Please, Sam," he begged and continued chest compressions. He listened for her to take a breath and repeated the action, counting to himself to keep the pace up.

Nat's soft cries, along with the crackling of the fire devouring the house, filled the air with rigid tension.

"Breathe, Sam. Breathe. I love you, sweetheart. Please breathe. Please." He continued to blow and pump her chest without a response. Minute after minute passed without a reaction from Sam. He growled and roared at the injustice of it all. He'd just gotten her back. How could life be so cruel? He blew into her lungs again.

She coughed, and he almost collapsed in relief.

Her pulse was weak, but he heard the faint wheezing of her body trying to get oxygen into her lungs.

Moments later, an ambulance, the fire department, Kane, and Zeno arrived. Paramedics rushed over to Sam and placed an oxygen mask over her nose and mouth. His gaze never strayed from Sam's limp body as the two men placed her on a gurney and lifted her.

"To our clinic," he instructed the shifter paramedics.

"Yes, sir." They carefully slid the gurney into the back of the ambulance.

He turned to find Kane and Zeno speaking to a fire department connection while Troy held Nat. The couple quickly rushed forward.

Riel was not wasting time. "I'm going to the clinic with them."

Nat nodded, tears streaming down her face. "We'll follow behind you."

Doctor Raven was waiting for them at the entrance when they arrived.

Sam was rushed into the intensive care unit for severe smoke inhalation and hooked up to a heart monitor and an oxygen tank. His gut clenched when he heard her cough, a dry, painful sound that broke his heart.

Raven patted his arm. "She'll be fine. I understand you gave her CPR?"

Riel nodded. If only she knew how terrified he was the entire time. "I did."

Raven smiled sadly. "We'll take good care of her. Why don't you wait outside while we monitor her, and once we're done you can come sit by her."

The thought of leaving her made his heart hurt, but he knew they had a job to do. He stared at Raven in the eyes. "I'll be outside. Call me if anything changes."

Troy and Nat sat in the waiting room along with Kane and Zeno. Minutes later, Sophia and Chase showed up. Sophia threw herself into Riel's arms in one of her sisterly displays of love.

"I'm so sorry. Is she okay?" Her concern was palpable, and Riel appreciated her for it. Chase gave him a brotherly hug and curled an arm around Sophia's waist.

Riel swallowed against the sand dunes residing in his throat. "She will be. She'd stopped breathing, but I gave her CPR and she's holding strong."

Chase nodded and squeezed Sophia into his side. "What happened?"

Nat sniffed through her tears. "I can tell you." She stepped forward. "More or less."

Everyone turned to her, and Riel wondered how the hell he'd left Sam for what must have been just a few moments only to come back and find her tied up inside a burning house.

"When Ry dropped her off, I told her I wanted to pick her brain for family history. She said she needed to get something at her house. She walked out saying she would be right back. She went to the house and came back with a small trunk.

"Then she ran back to lock the front door. After I made her sandwich, I noticed she didn't come back as quickly as the first time. I ran out to find the house engulfed in flames. I called Troy, and when I was talking to him Ry showed up."

Riel picked it up from there. "The house is

gone. I was lucky to get her out in time." Agony lanced his chest when he thought of what could've happened had he not gone back. Something had nagged at him to return, and so he'd turned around before reaching Kane.

"We still don't know who's trying to hurt her?" Chase glanced from Riel to the other enforcers.

"No," Kane said. "There are a lot of shady family members to go through. Our main suspects are Juan Junior and Kurt Danitelli, but Junior's been missing in action for a few days, which makes it harder, and we're still getting information about Danitelli."

Riel finally realized that's what Kane had wanted to see him about. Just because Juan Junior was missing didn't mean he wasn't behind what was happening to Sam.

As for Danitelli, there were mob ties, and he needed to know how badly he might want Sam dead.

"We'll call in others to help look into her family," Chase said to Riel.

He nodded to Chase.

Riel turned to face Raven.

She squeezed his bicep. "She's doing well. She was drugged, so it makes it even more important that we keep her under close observation until she's awake and conscious."

"What do you mean she was drugged?" Riel roared.

Chase gripped his shoulder in an attempt to get him to calm down.

Raven nodded, unperturbed by Riel's outburst, and pursed her lips. "I'm running blood tests to figure out exactly what it is, but preliminary tests show she was given a heavy dose of muscle relaxers. Had the dosage been any stronger, we could have been facing some serious problems. It was only enough to put her to sleep. She won't be awake probably until tomorrow, if not the day after."

An overwhelming rage consumed Riel from the inside.

"You can see her now but keep it brief. She's not going to wake up. It's still helpful for patients to hear their loved ones when they're asleep, so go ahead and speak to her." Raven walked toward a nurse waiting for her.

Riel turned to Nat. "Come on."

He knew she felt guilty, and he wanted to help appease her concern. None of what happened was Nat's fault, and she shouldn't carry that type of burden.

As they walked into the room, his gaze wandered over Sam's pale face. Thin plastic tubes had been placed inside her nose.

The long, dark curls of her hair had been pushed back from her face, and a blue hospital gown replaced her clothing.

Loud wheezing sounds came from her chest. It bothered him that her throat was so raw and she still had such a hard time breathing, but he was glad to see her chest move up and down with every breath.

Bandages covered her wrists. When she was brought to the hospital her hands and wrists had been bleeding from the rope she'd been tied with.

Nat strode to the bed and grab Sam's bandaged hand, speaking quietly in a wobbly voice. "I'm so sorry, Sam. If I hadn't—"

"This isn't your fault," he told her. "No one could have known this would happen. I'm sure Sam wouldn't want you to feel guilty."

Nat nodded and wiped her cheeks with the backs of her hands. She bent, kissed Sam's forehead, and then turned to Riel. "Sam's really special. Please, please, love her with all you've got, because that's how she loves you. She needs happiness in her life."

Nat walked toward the door and stopped. "I'm not sure if Sam understands what a mate means to your kind, but she knows what love means. And it means everything."

Riel stood in silence listening to the sounds of the machines beep. Emotions ran rampant inside him for his mate. Anger, fear, love, and pain all mingled to make a cocktail of frustration he'd never felt before. He walked toward her and sat by the bed.

For those endless moments when she'd stopped breathing, his heart had ceased to beat. Even if she wasn't his mate, he'd still want her. She'd captured his heart the first moment he'd seen her. His mate was not going to be hurt again. And he wasn't letting her go.

TWENTY-THREE

When she opened her eyes, the first thing Sam noticed was the darkness. She was in a hospital room, and Riel was sleeping on a chair beside her bed. She grinned.

His head lolled forward in repose. The slight beard growth and messy brown hair made him look so sexy. A white T-shirt did a poor job concealing his bulging muscles beneath.

Memories of how she ended up in the hospital assailed her brain. He'd saved her, again. If she didn't already love him, she surely did now. The man had gone into a burning house to get her out.

She tested her voice. "Ry." The low croak was barely audible, but his head shot up.

He moved forward and caressed her cheek with one hand. "Don't talk. Doctor Raven said your throat is going to hurt for a while. Let me get you some ice." He moved toward a table and filled a plastic cup with ice chips.

Trying to make herself comfortable, she turned her head to the side rail and searched for a button to lift the bed to a sitting position. Once she was finally up, she smiled. He sat on the edge of the bed and passed her the cup.

The cool comfort of the ice chips going down her throat rivaled the pleasure from eating the best ice cream in the world.

Several chips later, she tried her voice again. "Thank you." No longer a weird trucker hack, her voice had the low, husky tone found in phone-sex operators.

She grinned, cleared her throat, and tried again. "Testing, testing. If you'd like for me to strip, press one now." When Riel's brows lifted, she laughed and then coughed. Crap, she should've known her lungs were still not ready for comedy hour.

He quirked his lips, but his frown was all concern. "How do you feel?"

"Better than I did the last time I saw you. The house?" Hopeful that something was salvaged, she bit her lip and waited.

He gave a sad shake of his head. "I'm sorry, sweetheart. It's all gone."

All of Ginny's memories evaporated because someone wanted to be rid of Sam. The only thing left was that trunk she'd taken to Riel's home. Ginny's home was the only place she'd ever really belonged.

Tears gathered in her eyes, and she blinked back the need to cry. Not only had she lost Ginny, but she'd lost a lifetime of memories with the only relative who had ever cared for her.

"It's okay. I know there was nothing you could do. Hell, you got me out alive. Thank you." She wrapped her arms around his neck and pulled him in for a hug.

The spiky hairs of his beard growth pinched at her skin when he sniffed her. He fluttered soft kisses over her neck and shoulder. Having his nose by her throat brought a measure of comfort she hadn't expected.

His soft rumble vibrated by her ear. "You don't need to thank me. I would never let anything happen to you. You're mine." And she was in full agreement. She was his, and he was hers.

The door flew open, startling her and Ry. Mr. Carson, her grandmother's lawyer, rushed in, wide-eyed and breathing heavily. "I came as soon as I heard. Samira, are you all right?"

She smiled at him. The lawyer was a great

man. She wished her grandmother would've hooked up with him. They could've made a great couple. She introduced the new visitor to Ry and they shook hands.

Mr. Carson said, "I'm glad she has someone to look over her and protect her." His brow raised and he turned toward her in the bed. "Maybe protect a bit more would be even better?"

A deep growl rumbled from Riel. The old man had insulted her mate's wolf, not to mention Riel. When he puffed his chest out, she decided to nip this potential fiasco in the bud.

"Sweetie," she said, immediately drawing her mate's attention, "would you mind getting me a juice from the hospital cafeteria? I could really use more liquid."

Ry gave her a nod and passed by Mr. Carson, never taking his eyes off the man. For good measure, he lifted his lip and growled. Sam sighed and rolled her eyes.

After the door closed, the lawyer took up her hand. "Are you sure you're all right? I stopped by the house for you to sign those papers, but I couldn't get any closer than a block with all the fire trucks and police. One of the nice women standing outside told me what happened and where you were."

"I'll be okay," she rasped.

"Do you know who did this?" he asked.

She shook her head. "They placed a bag over my head so I couldn't see."

Carson patted her and took a deep breath. "If we find out it's one of your family members, not only will they be disinherited, but will go to prison."

"Do you really think my aunts or uncle are capable of this?" She'd been gone a long time. People change. Maybe they were worse than she thought.

Carson replied, "I don't know. Ginny didn't talk much about them. She was embarrassed of them, I believe."

"Mr. Carson," she started, "will you do me a favor and call a family meeting like you did for the reading of the will? I think it's time to confront the family before this goes any farther."

"Great idea. I'll get on that as soon I leave and will text the time and place to everyone." He sighed as if to calm himself. "Well, it's good to see you're not injured too terribly." She gave him a big smile hoping to show she was fine, for the most part.

"I should be going," he said. "There's always work to do." At that moment, his phone rang. He pulled it from his pocket and waved bye as he walked out of the room.

TWENTY-FOUR

Riel stomped his way to the cafeteria. He wasn't stupid enough to not realize Sam gave him this errand to get him out of the room.

And dammit, he knew he should've been at the house protecting her. He'd told her not to leave, but did she listen? *Noooo.*

With a sigh, he sucked up his attitude and swallowed it. He'd love his mate no matter what she did. But nothing was said about killing her. He could ring her luscious, tasty neck right now. Thinking about that made his pants fit tighter. Damn, not the place or time for that.

He picked out an apple juice drink and paid twice the amount it would've cost in the grocery store. Typical nowadays.

Coming down the hall to Sam's room, he heard Carson's voice. Sounded like he was on the phone with the pauses. He stopped at the corner to listen.

"She'll be fine," Carson said and paused. "No, she doesn't know who, but when I find out—" Pause. "Of course, it's someone in the family—" Pause. "Don't worry. I have it all worked out."

Riel heard the elevator ding and that ended the conversation.

What did the man have all worked out?

* * *

After several long days in the hospital, when she finally returned to Riel's house, the first thing she did was shower. She carried the grime of the world on her skin.

Her amazing man had gotten Nat to buy her new clothes. They were situated in his closet waiting for her. Everything she needed of a personal nature sat by his toiletries in his bedroom.

Remembering Sophia's words about Riel wanting their mating to be Sam's choice, she decided not to wait any longer.

She'd almost died twice, and the reality was that anything could happen. There were no guarantees in life. Why stop from acknowledging how she felt because some arbitrary set amount of time hadn't passed? Who said there was a right time to tell someone you loved them? All she knew was that she wasn't going to go another day without him knowing the extent of her feelings.

She was in love with him, and there was no way she'd live the rest of her life without him knowing. Aside from her feelings, her body and hormones were wreaking havoc with her mental stability. She was still horny as hell, and her body craved him in the worst way.

She put on her new robe and waited for him to return to the bedroom. The soft, silky material reminded her of all the clothes she'd lost. Her entire collection of sexy lingerie had gone up in flames.

She'd just have to start a new one.

Excitement dashed through her when she thought of buying new sexy clothing and modeling it for Ry. Tying her hair up in a knot, she paced the bedroom. Footsteps sounded down the hallway and headed her way, sending a rush of eagerness through her.

Riel walked through the door with a tray. He'd cooked for her again. Could the man be any more perfect? Their gazes met and held. Lust flared in his eyes, spiking her temperature and making her heart flip.

While he placed the tray on the dresser, she tried to think of the best way to proceed. After debating for a moment, she decided honesty was her best course of action.

His nostrils flared, and he sniffed. She grinned as the color of his eyes turned into liquid gold. He knew she was aroused. Evidence of her desire dripped down her thighs. The fire that made her pussy clench and moisten had given off her needy state.

Fascinated, her stomach flipped when his facial muscles tightened and his jaw clenched. With a leisurely stroll, she made her way toward him.

"Sam…"

She opened the tie around her waist holding her robe closed. The robe slipped down her body with a quiet swoosh and landed on the wood floor in a puddle of silky material. Her nipples pebbled into tight points, and another wave of moisture dripped from her pussy.

She draped her hands on the hard muscles of his stomach. Each of the tiny squares in his abs beckoned for her to lick at the tight skin. She smiled at his soft growl.

"I love you." Saying the words wasn't as hard as she thought.

His eyes widened. "Are you sure?" He gave

her a silly grin. "You don't need to profess love for me just because I'm amazing in bed," he joked.

She laughed. Here she was, opening her heart to him, and he was making jokes. She couldn't get angry, because she knew that behind his joke, he was nervous over her declaration. "I'm positive. I wouldn't say it if I wasn't. I love you. You're mine and...if you want me, I'm yours."

TWENTY-FIVE

He pulled her into his arms and consumed her with a kiss so hot, it made her skin sizzle. The kiss was hard and rough. It invaded her senses. He caressed down her spine, farther to her hips, and settled on her ass.

He grabbed her cheeks and lifted her off the ground, her pussy ending up level with his cock. He stroked his denim-covered shaft into the seam of her pussy. An explosion of passion took hold, leaving her breathless and panting. She rubbed her nipples over his chest.

He put her on her feet and cupped her face with his hands. His gaze spoke of passion, possession, and a feeling she knew lived in her heart for him, love. "Sam, I love you. There are no words to tell you how much. Of course, I want you. I'll always want you. There's no one else for me."

Happiness unfurled in her heart between the kisses he rained on her lips and face. When he let go of her head, she curled her arms around his neck and rubbed her nose on his smooth jaw.

"There's no other man for me...just you." She licked his chin and nibbled on his neck. "You're my mate, and I'm yours. We just need to make it official."

She grazed her teeth over the galloping pulse on his throat. "Bite me, baby."

He growled over the curve of her shoulder. "Thank god. I don't know how much longer I could have waited. I mean I could've waited as long as you needed, but I've been dying to stake my claim. You're mine."

She raked her nails down his chest and lifted his T-shirt. All those clothes had to come off immediately. She tugged on the material and growled. It was taking too damn long to get him undressed. He chuckled and tore the offensive fabric from his body, and she sighed.

He dipped his head and kissed her, another wave of ferocious mating of the tongues and lips.

Urgency to have him in her body pushed her to open his jeans, shove her hand down, and grab his cock in a tight grip. His breath hissed out in a groan. She pushed the jeans down and pumped his shaft in a slow glide from root to tip.

"God, Sam. You're so fucking hot." His deep gravelly voice heightened her desire.

"Fuck me, Ry," she whimpered. "Fuck me. Mate me. Make me yours."

He growled, toed off his jeans, and picked her up in his arms. He laid her on the bed carefully, as if she were a porcelain doll. They kissed again, softer, but still just as needy. She spread her legs for him and summoned him with the crook of a finger.

Heat swelled inside her. He inhaled and licked his lips. "You smell delicious." Lust shot down to her wet folds as he groaned. "And I just know you're going to taste even better."

He pounced on the bed, wrapped his arms around her legs, and immediately fastened his lips around her clit. Her hands flew to the short spikes of his hair. He swiped his thick tongue mercilessly over her clit.

She writhed and thrashed on the bed. "Yes, yes, yes, yes, yes…"

He thrusts two digits into her sex and curved them inside her pussy, tickling her G-spot at the same time he grazed his teeth over her clit. A spasm took hold, and she shattered so fast, it left her breathless. Lost to the throes of her climax, she screamed his name.

He flipped her on her stomach, ass high in

the air and legs wide open. He fondled her pussy, sliding his fingers in, out, and around her wet folds. She gasped, passion tightening her nipples and making her pussy clench. She glanced over her shoulder. He bit his lip and caressed her ass with what looked like adoration.

She groaned and hung her head. Holding the sheets in a death grip, she moaned as the broad head of his cock penetrated her slick heat. He gripped her hips, stretching her pussy walls, until he was balls-deep inside her.

Looking for more than just penetration, she wiggled and whimpered at the fantastic feel of his cock grazing her from inside. He tightened his hold on her hips, pulled back, and thrust into her in a fast slide. She turned her head just as he thrust into her again. He pulled back and slammed into her harder. She groaned and fisted the sheets tighter.

"Do you like that?" He impaled her again. "Like it when I fuck you from behind?"

"Yes, yes. Please."

"Please what? What do you need, my sexy mate?" The low growl and his feral features made her pussy squeeze at his cock.

"Fuck me harder, faster. Give me more!"

His wicked grin made the heat inside her expand through every cell and nerve ending.

Hair sprouted on his face. She became fascinated. His features turned wild, untamed and almost feral with intensity. Inside her pussy, his cock thickened and grew.

"Mine," his voice claimed.

"Yes. Yours." Her breath hitched. She hung her head and lowered her front to lie flat on the bed just as he seemed to let go of his control.

He pulled back and hammered into her in harsh drives. Every thrust and pull of his thickened cock dragged loud, harsh moans out of her throat. Skin slapping skin, her moans and his growls were the only noises in the room.

Fire filled her pussy with each slam of his cock. In. Out. Her ass lifted off the bed with each one. "Mine." He ground his cock into her pussy again.

"God, yes!" A ball of tension grew inside her womb. Her pussy fluttered, and her back bowed. He snarled and dropped on all fours over her, caging her. Sweat turned the slide of his body over hers into a sensual glide of flesh on flesh. He licked the back of her shoulder. She moaned and propelled back into each of his thrusts, pushing him even farther into her pussy.

Holding himself over her with one arm, he moved a hand between her thighs and squeezed her clit between two fingers. She gasped, tensed, and when his canines dug into her shoulder, her world exploded. Her pussy clenched around his cock and squeezed as she came.

Unbelievably, it felt as if his cock grew even more inside her pussy. He slowed the pummeling thrusts, tensed above her, and snarled while still biting her shoulder. Hot semen filled her womb in multiple jerks. He continued to come for long moments with his teeth still embedded in her flesh.

Attached, they fell to the side on the mattress. He wrapped his hands around her waist, his cock jerked in her pussy, and he licked at her shoulder. She panted air into her lungs and closed her eyes.

TWENTY-SIX

Sam woke with a start. Riel's side of the bed was empty. She blinked and climbed out of bed. She checked her phone quickly for messages and read the text from Mr. Carson about the family meeting at their offices in a few days. He wasn't joking when he'd said he get on it. She'd worry about that later.

Moonlight drifted in through the window, and no other noise came from inside the house. A quiet splashing noise made her walk to the bedroom window. The moon and backyard lights illuminated the large pool.

Riel's lithe body cut through the water like a missile. Awed at the speed and precision of his moves, she stared until she realized she could just go down there and join him. She wrapped her robe around her naked body and headed downstairs.

With every step she took, she thought of the amazing things he'd done to her. Desire flared and made her quicken her steps. A soft breeze caressed her skin, ruffling her loose hair.

The splashing noises grew until she was standing by the water, watching his muscles ripple with every move he made. Heat grew inside her, lust shot through her veins, and her pussy dripped in need. She disrobed and walked down the pool steps. Cool water kissed her heated skin and made her moan in delight.

When he got to the far end of the pool and took a breath, he turned in the water. She smiled and went under. Water surrounded her, and after a few strokes she came up against a wall of flesh. Under the water, she scanned his body. His cock was fully erect and in her face. She used her last bit of oxygen to wrap her lips around his dick and take a quick suck, then she went up for air.

He curled his hands around her waist and pulled her flush against his body. She snaked her arms around his shoulders, grazing her nails on the back of his neck. Hunger for him made her whimper. She pulled his head down and immediately ran her tongue over his wet lips. Stimulated into desperation, she sucked on his neck and bit his shoulder. He squeezed her ass and held her pussy over his cock.

She wrapped her legs around his waist until

his cock kissed her entrance.

He dropped her over his cock in a slow glide.

When she wiggled her hips, he groaned. "Baby, I'm going crazy for you."

She panted and licked his neck. "Can we go crazy together?" Her body burned for him. "Fuck me, my big, sexy wolf." She grazed her teeth over his shoulders and nibbled the wet flesh.

"Jesus, Sam. I love you, sweetheart." He kissed her softly on the lips.

Her heart expanded with love for her man. "I love you, too."

He guided her body up and down his shaft. His thick cock rubbed her insides repeatedly, driving her passion to relentless heights.

He attached to her breast, twirling his tongue on her nipple and then biting on the tender tip. Mini- explosions went off in her womb, and her pussy fluttered. He let go of her breast, growled, and rammed her up and down his cock in swift moves. She moaned.

Her pussy clasped around his cock, and she sucked on his shoulder. Completely lost to the throes of passion, she bit down and broke skin. Her orgasm tore through her at light speed. She screamed and trembled with every ripple of pleasure that coursed through her body.

He shouted her name in a growl she almost didn't make out as he dug his fingers into her waist. One final ram into her with his cock and he shuddered. His shaft thickened and filled her womb with his essence.

They stayed together in the water holding each other. She laid her head on his shoulder, facing away from his throat. She held him tightly, linking her legs behind his ass, sighing. His cock was still deep inside her, and if she had her wish he'd stay there forever.

It had been in the front of her mind to ask about the threat against her. "What are we going to do about the person or persons trying to kill me?" Her words were soft, low. There was no need to say anything louder. His enhanced hearing would pick up on what she said.

He slipped them to the stairs in the pool and sat down with her over him, on his lap. She hugged him tighter as he wrapped his arms around her back in a protective gesture. Her heart expanded with feelings for him.

"Don't worry, sweetheart. Whoever is doing this will have to go through me to get to you." His angry growl made her feel even more protected.

She nibbled on her lip. "What if they are after Ginny's money and nothing we do stops them?"

"Sam—" He sounded ready to argue.

"No, listen. I don't want you to be in the middle of something that could get you hurt." The last thing she needed was to lose the one man that made her happy now that she'd found him.

"I'm not the one in danger. You are." His voice was quiet, serious.

"I know that, but what if by protecting me, you get hurt in the process? I couldn't live with myself."

He growled softly. "I'm sorry, sweetheart. You're going to have to live with it, because I'm not going anywhere. Wherever you go, I go. I don't intend on letting anyone else try to kill you."

She'd never be able to live with herself if she allowed something to happen to him. She would just have to make sure she looked out for him while he looked out for her. "I promise not to take any unnecessary risks, Ry. Can you promise the same?"

"Hell no! You come first."

"Please, Ry. Can you just promise to be careful? Don't be bullheaded about this. I will do my part, and you do yours. We can stay safe and find the people behind this."

He sighed. "Sam, you need to understand that if it comes down to your life or mine, yours always comes first."

She jerked her head up so fast, she almost got whiplash. "No! Don't say that!"

He nodded. "It's true. I can't live without you, so I can't let anything happen to you."

She shook her head. "And you think I can live without you? That wouldn't work at all."

"All I know is that if anyone tries to lay a hand on you again, I'm going to tear them to shreds." He tightened his hold on her waist.

She dropped her head back on his shoulder. A sick sense of foreboding filled her stomach. His chin rubbed over her wet hair and she closed her eyes and sighed. A second later, she snapped them open and yanked her head up so fast she hit him in the chin with her skull. They both groaned in pain. She rubbed her head with one hand and his chin with the other.

"I'm sorry. I'm sorry. It's just I just remembered something I'd completely forgotten about!"

"What?" He laughed. She wasn't sure if it was because she was so excited or because she looked like a maniac.

She started bouncing on his lap.

"Ginny's trunk!" She stopped bouncing when his cock thickened. He became rock-hard inside her again. Well, damn. Her whimpers spoke for her. They would check out Ginny's trunk...in a minute, after she had her mate one more time.

TWENTY-SEVEN

Riel carried Sam up to their bed. His house was her house now, so there was no need for her to go anywhere. His mate belonged with him. They reached the bedroom, and he put her down.

She ran to the bathroom and came out wearing a towel over her hair in a turban style, coupled with a different robe around her body. Her other robe had gotten wet on their two attempts to leave the yard.

She blew him a kiss. Taking quick strides, she headed for the dresser where he'd placed the small trunk for her. Once he'd put on boxers, he met her on the bed. She'd already opened the trunk and flipped it, emptying its contents on the blue comforter. Papers, letters, official documents, and pictures spread before them.

"Oh, wow. Look at this, Ry! There are pictures. I thought all the photos had burned in the fire, but Ginny had some in here." Her excitement was palpable.

He picked up a handful of photos. His attention was caught by a woman with a duplicate of Sam's face. Her mother. He didn't need for her to tell him. It was obvious from the physical similarities they shared.

He saw the back of the next photo first. It read "Susana and Korr." Riel flipped it to the image of the couple. Susana was clearly very young, possibly a teenager. The man in the shot appeared to be older, and Riel knew he was the shifter. He knew of a Korr that had been an enforcer to Chase's father when they were kids.

His mate was going through photos of other family members. Her gaze darted up to his face. "What's wrong? What did you find?"

It wasn't his right to hold anything from her, so he passed her the photo. His focus never strayed from her face. His gut clenched, watching the play of emotions rushing over her features. Her eyes widened while she stared at the woman in the photograph.

"Oh my god. That's my mother." She sounded surprised.

"Hadn't you seen her before? Don't you

remember your mother?"

A look of pure desolation passed over her face, and she shook her head. "No. Ginny showed me one picture of her, but she told me it hurt her to look. I didn't ask because she'd given me so much, but I always wanted to see more pictures of her." She nibbled her lip. "Maybe that's my father."

"You didn't know your father?"

"No. Ginny only said he'd died and that she didn't want to discuss my parents because it was too painful. Just the mention of my mother had her in tears for days. Do you think this man is my father?"

He nodded. "Yes. I also think he's your shifter link."

"But how can you know?"

"Korr was an enforcer for Chase's father before our time." He continued to watch her stare at the photo.

Her finger trailed over the images, as if wishing to touch the people on the paper. "What happened to him?"

"He was killed during a fight with puma shifters. They ambushed the town, and it was a bloody war. Everyone heard about it. We were little kids. Chase was ten, and I was around five. We were protected to ensure the survival of the pack." He lifted a hand to her cheek and wiped away the tears running down her face. "I'm sorry."

She sniffed. "Why? Don't worry. It's just sad to see a photo of them together and know I never got to know either of them."

He frowned, remembering her earlier words. "What do you mean you didn't get to know her?"

She shook her head, put the photo to the side, and started searching through documents. "She died right after I was born. Something happened and…" She stared at the paper in her hand, her face frozen, eyes wide, and mouth agape.

"What is it?" He moved closer to glance at the paper in her hand.

"It's a document stating my mother was hospitalized for a mental breakdown six months before my birth." She scanned the document and gasped. "She was pregnant at the time and was suffering from mental illness and severe depression from loss."

"That's so sad."

Sam's gaze met his. "What would make her lose her mind with grief?"

"The loss of her mate?"

She glanced back down at the sheet. "When

was the date of that war?"

He gave her the information. She ruffled through pages. Her moves were frantic, her hands shaking with each letter she skimmed through. After a few letters she stopped, read, and covered her mouth. A muffled cry sounded behind her hand. He pulled the sheet from her grip and read.

Dear Mom,

I'm sorry you are so concerned for me. I'm trying to lose this overwhelming depression at the loss of Korr, but nothing seems to help.

They've given me some new drug that's supposed to help with the hallucinations and loss of appetite. I feel so selfish knowing my child grows in my womb, and I can't find it in me to be happy. Life has dealt me a blow I never expected.

To lose my husband, the father of my child, the only man I have ever loved, and my mate has pushed me past the edge of living into the realm of existing. I breathe, eat, and survive just to ensure my daughter will live, but the truth is, I can easily lie here and die.

My will to live is gone, and nothing is helping to bring it back. Please forgive me for asking this of you, Mother. Please take care of my Sam if anything happens to me.

Love,

Susana

TWENTY-EIGHT

What her mother suffered would've been normal among shifters. The loss of a mate could mean the end to a shifter. Symptoms ranged anywhere from depression, anxiety, loss of enjoyment in life, weight loss, and some even went as far as suicide.

Riel glanced up at Sam, and his heart broke for her. He pulled her shaking body into his arms and held her while she sobbed openly.

Every time her breath hitched it was as if a knife was shoved into his heart. He wanted to make things better for her but didn't know how. The towel in her hair fell to the side, leaving her long dark curls hanging damp. He used the towel to wipe her face and did the only thing he could think to show her she wasn't alone: he kissed her.

A soft flutter of his lips over hers. He held

her face and caressed her soft cheeks with his thumbs.

"I'm sorry. I've turned into an emotional rollercoaster." The sorrow in her voice made him even more determined to stand by her side.

"It's okay, sweetheart." She grabbed another letter from the pile. They read it together.

Dear Mom,

I'm scared. I'm not sure what's going on, but the drugs they're giving me are making me really sick. I feel as if something isn't right with the baby. She's slowed her movements, and I asked the doctor if he could stop the medication, but he refused.

Please, Mom, take me out of here. Sam will be born any day, and I don't think this medicine is helping me as much as it's hurting her. I can't live with the thought that I caused her any pain because of my weakness. Get me out of this place, Mom. I want my baby with you.

I know my time is short. They don't think I know, but my kidneys aren't well. It's a side effect of this medicine. I'm sure you thought not telling me would make things easier on me, but now all I can think of is my Samira.

If you ever loved me, do this for me. Let me have my baby out of here.

Your daughter,

Susana

"I can't believe Ginny would let her own daughter sit in a hospital getting pumped with a medication that made her sicker."

Sam shook her head, lifting a newer letter. It was addressed to her. Once again, they both read it together.

Dear Sam,

I'm sick and will probably die before you come home. How sad that I was too much of a coward to tell this to you in person, but I loved you so much, as much as I loved my Susana.

When your father was killed, Susana was so grief-stricken she had a hard time coping and moving on. If I hadn't known for sure my husband was fully human, I would have believed she was a shifter in loss of her mate.

Your Aunt Margarita never cared for Susana or her mate Korr. I'm not sure if it was because she'd tried to gain his attention but never succeeded or if it was just plain jealousy.

Whatever, all I know is that I made a mistake. I listened to Maggie. She mentioned a doctor who was using new drugs to help people with severe mental illness.

Until that point, I didn't think Susana was that sick, but then she started having hallucinations. You were already in her belly, so I needed to look out for you. It wasn't until you were almost born that I found out the drugs Susana was given were a powerful combination of dangerous compounds no one had ever mixed.

I brought Susana home, but she passed away shortly after you were born. It was after she was home that I found out she never had hallucinations until she started getting treated by that doctor.

It made me feel even guiltier for putting my own daughter in the devil's hands. I promised her I'd look after you. My guilt and shame have been mine to bear. All I can ask is for you to forgive me for not ensuring your mother's health when I had the chance.

It's my hope that asking Riel, your mate, to give you the time to spread your wings as you wish will at least give you the space to learn to handle being a shifter's mate.

Yes, he is your mate, Sam. He told me the moment he saw you the first time and I didn't have it in me to let you go so soon. Your mother loved Korr, and I know you and Riel belong together. You may not shift, but the link is there.

There's a bond between you that no one can take away. Even I can see it. You can trust him. He'll love and care for you when I'm gone.

Love,

Ginny

Riel glanced at Sam. She was still staring blankly at the letter. He knew she was suffering, and his wolf pushed him to do something to make her feel better. But what? He couldn't change the past.

His gut clenched. The grief and loneliness in her eyes were enough to make a knot form in his throat. She put all the letters and photos back in the trunk in complete quietness. Then she lifted the trunk and put it on the floor.

She removed her robe, sliding out of the silky material in drawn-out moves. He gulped. She crawled to him, completely naked.

His cock hardened instantly, and he felt like a sick bastard. "Sam?"

Here she was going through this sad discovery of her past, and he was ready to lay her on the bed and worship every inch of her luscious body.

She sat on the back of her feet and placed a finger over his lips. "Shhh." Her soft, sad smile was his undoing. "Make love to me, Ry. I don't want to feel alone anymore."

He cupped her face in his hands. "You'll never be alone again, sweetheart. I'm always going to be by your side."

"I know. But I have a lot to think about, and I can't do it with the heat I feel inside urging me at every moment to have you filling my body. You have to help me. I don't want to leave this room until my body no longer screams for you to take me every second of the day, okay?" She moved the finger over his mouth and trailed it over his lips. "I need you to make this burning stop."

What the fuck could he say to that? If his mate wanted him to make love to her then he would. "Sam—"

"I'm all yours, Ry."

And that's exactly what he did for the following several days. He ignored all but the most important calls and explained to others his need to be home with her. Once the word heat came up, everyone understood and backed off.

Food, sex, and bonding with his mate were all that mattered to him. When they finally emerged from his home, he couldn't stop the satisfied grin covering his face. Their mate bond had strengthened into a tangible link that he'd never felt for anyone else.

He took in Sam's sexy body as she floated in the pool, naked. He was glad he'd built a high fence over the front yard. The only way to see into his backyard had been through Sam's backyard, but now that the house had burned, he'd had the side leading to his closed off. Privacy was important to him.

The ringing of his phone made him glance down at the name on the screen. Kane. He sat up on the lounger and pressed the button to answer the call.

"What's going on?" He knew Kane was investigating the family, so if he was calling, he probably had new information for him.

"Sorry to interrupt your time with Sam, Ry. We've found some interesting information on Sam's Aunt Cecilia. She's got a young man living with her, but he's sleeping with another woman. Since you were the one that got the scent of the man off Sam, I need you to come check him out."

TWENTY-NINE

Ry narrowed his eyes. "What about the other aunts?"

"Maggie and Luisa. Yeah, we're still doing background on them. But there is a lot of shit in this family. Maggie appears to just be a miserable old bitch. She keeps a strict schedule so following up on her shouldn't be too hard. We're still probing into her husband, Danitelli's affairs and business dealings. He's a slippery one. Luisa is last on our list after her."

A low growl worked up Riel's throat. He'd been dying to get his hands on the person that had tied Sam to the bed to burn.

"I'll be there soon." He didn't want to leave Sam alone, plus the family meeting at the lawyer's office that Sam mentioned was in an hour. He could be at Kane's and back in plenty of time.

"Where are you going?" she asked and toweled her body dry.

His eyes drank in every single sexy curve of her beautiful body. He pulled her on his lap and kissed her. "I need to see Kane. I'll have Troy come watch you."

She shook her head and kissed him on the nose. "Nope."

"What do you mean 'nope'?"

She curled her arms around his neck, kissed the shell of his ear, and ran a tongue over the rim. "I mean, nope. I'm going to visit Sophia and take the papers from my mom's medical stay. She wanted to see if she could figure out why I can't shift, and I want to know more about the drug they gave her." Her eyes filled with sorrow. "I need to know for my own peace of mind. You understand, right?"

He did. It wasn't hard for him to see how much it meant to her. "But, my love, have you forgotten your family powwow?"

She groaned. "I'm trying my best to forget my whole family much less our meeting." She sighed. "You're right. Drop me off at Sophia's, do your thing, then pick me up and we'll go from there."

After changing, Sam clutched all the relevant papers and shoved them into her new tote bag. She ran down the stairs knowing she'd left poor Ry waiting. He turned to her at the doorway, his face full of worry.

At Sophia's house, he sat idle in his SUV until Sophia opened the door and led her inside. He waved and drove away slowly. Talk about paranoid.

"You think that's bad? Chase won't even let me go anywhere without a driver. He thinks I'm just going to pass out behind the wheel," Sophia complained.

Sam's gaze went back to the other woman, and that's when she noticed the dark circles under Sophia's eyes. "Are you okay?" The pretty geneticist appeared to be sick.

Sophia beamed. "I'm pregnant. It makes me really tired." Didn't pregnancy make all women tired? "I'm different," Sophia said, reading her mind. "I get more tired than most women. I can sleep for days. At least this time it's not twins, or I really would be sleeping for days." She sighed and motioned Sam inside.

Wow. Would that happen to her?

Sophia answered almost like she'd read her thoughts. "I don't think that would happen to you, so don't worry. Most other shifter-pregnant women don't need as much rest as I do. Although you'll find you do need more than your usual amount of sleep."

"You're different?"

"Yes. I am a dual shifter, and so it takes a little more out of me."

Sam stared at the petite brunette. "You can turn into two different animals?"

She nodded. "Yes, and it really is quite fun, except for the being exhausted during pregnancy part."

That was way too much to take in for all the crazy stuff happening lately. "I brought some papers I found inside Ginny's trunk."

They headed to the living room where two cots held the twins.

"Should we be in here?" Sam whispered.

Sophia laughed. "Yeah. They can sleep through an earthquake. Plus, I can't leave them alone yet. Raven is getting me a nurse to help around here with them, but that's not for another week. Until then, I'm on my own."

"Wait. You said you have dual animals inside you."

Sophia bent over Selena and moved the clear pink pacifier away from her face. "That's right."

"So what are your babies, one animal or the other?"

Sophia grinned, her expression bright and excited. "They're dual shifters as well. It looks like Shane might be the first wolf/lion shifter born to an alpha wolf. If he turns out to be alpha in both, it can prove really interesting."

Sam was amazed. She couldn't wait to see if cute little Shane would be a dual leader one day.

Sophia groaned and glanced down at her smartphone. She pressed buttons and grinned. "See what I mean. Chase texts me every hour on the hour wanting to know how I'm feeling. Paranoia at its best." She laughed. "It's okay, though. We had some big scares in the past, so I don't hold his concern against him."

Sam remembered Ry's protectiveness. It seemed all of the shifter males went overboard ensuring their mate's safety.

She sat on a dark chocolate-colored leather sofa and passed papers to Sophia. "These are the documents I came across. I'm not sure what they mean, but it may be the reason why I'm not a shifter."

Sophia read through the documents, and a wave of nausea hit Sam. Her nerves made the anxiety inside her grow into a sick churning.

"I see."

"Well?"

"Do you know if there's anything with the name of the drug? That would've really helped."

Sam thought back, but all she'd left behind was an invoice from the hospital. She didn't recall seeing a drug named there, but maybe she'd missed it. "I'll check again. So you can't tell from this if this was what caused me to be this way?"

Sophia gave a soft shake of her head. "No, Sam. I'm sorry. I want to tell you it was caused by whatever they gave your mother, but the reality is, it could just be a mutated gene. For all we know, your body rejected the gene that allowed the change, and that's why you're not a shifter. I'm not sure, but I will find out for you."

Sam's spirits plummeted. She'd hoped Sophia would be able to put her concerns to bed.

"Let me get another sample of your blood, and I'll look into different drugs I know can cause these kinds of effects, okay?"

She nodded and guarded the children while Sophia brought the items necessary to obtain a blood sample.

"Don't worry, Sam. I will figure this out."

"Thank you. I really want to know what caused that difference in me versus everyone else."

THIRTY

"You ready for this?" Ry asked her as they sat in the truck in the parking lot at Carson & Willis Attorneys' office.

Of course, she wasn't. She'd never faced all of them together in one room, not even as a kid. The reading of the will was the first time, and she tried to hide at that.

"There's no choice," she said. "This shit has to stop right now. We've already lost everything in Grandmother's home."

He leaned toward her, she met him halfway. He placed a hot kiss on her. "You're amazing. Have I told you that yet?"

Her phone rang and she pulled it from her purse. It was Mr. Carson. "Hi, Sam. I'm running a bit late. Stuck at the train." That had been a pain in the ass forever. The train seemed to always come at the most inopportune time.

"No problem, Mr. Carson. We're all inside." Well, not really, but she was working on it. Sam took a deep breath and blew it out. "Let's do this."

Before getting out of the truck, Ry's phone buzzed. He glanced at the screen. "It's Chase. Gotta take it."

She nodded and continued to get climb out. Shoulders back and head held high, she strode into the office and the meeting room. Her family was back, and they didn't look happy. But then, when did they ever?

Before she could say anything, her uncle hollered across the room. "Well, if it isn't my little cuz," Juan Junior spat.

Oh, great. Just what she needed. "What is your problem, Junior?" She was tired of his condescending ways.

Juan Junior snarled like the very animals he hated. His gaze moved to the door Sam had entered. Sam turned to see no one. She thought Mr. Carson had arrived.

Juan's face was blotchy and his eyes red-rimmed as if he'd been drinking all night. He exuded the disgusting smell of sweat, vomit, and liquor. "So now you're consorting with animals just like that whore mother of yours, I see."

Anger bubbled up inside her. His words were meant to hurt, and they'd done the job. She wanted to hit him. She growled and moved, not realizing she'd done it until he was only a foot away from her. "Don't you dare speak of my mother! She never did anything to any of you."

"She was a filthy whore that liked to get fucked by animals. You don't think that bothered us? It made us all look like depraved fools!" Juan yelled at her as if she were a piece of trash in his way.

Her temper snapped. "My father wasn't an animal, you asshole!" Her voice rose with her temper. "They were in love. She was his mate, and he was hers. Do you even know what love is, you self-serving, no good son of a bitch?!" By the end of her speech she was screaming the words at the top of her lungs.

Juan's face reddened to a deep burgundy, and his eyes narrowed with hate. "You little bitch. You think you can talk to me like that and keep my money? That's my inheritance Ginny put in your name."

"Yeah? Well, guess what, primo?" she drawled in the same hillbilly whine Juan used, "I'm giving it all away to charity. Every single cent is going to the poor and the needy."

She smirked at his outraged features. "Yeah. Every...single...penny." She punctuated each word to drive the point home. He wouldn't get a single dime if she had to burn it all. She was beyond caring.

Juan had gone too far by speaking ill of her parents. She continued. "Te lo prometo. I swear I will make sure nothing, not one cent, goes to your greedy fat hands. I hope you rot in hell without a pot to piss in, you bastard."

She didn't see the danger until it was too late. He jerked a meaty hand toward her face, shoving her backward with a loud slap. She fell, slamming against the conference table.

Pain lanced her face and made her eyes water. She groaned and lifted a hand to block other attacks but be grabbed her by her T-shirt and slapped her across the face again. Needles of torture shot through her cheek and jaw.

The taste of copper filled her mouth, and she knew she bled. She tried to get loose from him, but his grip was tight, and he was huge compared to her. She kicked and punched to no avail.

"Help me!" she yelled at her aunts who stood on the other side of the room, jaws hanging down. Cecilia snapped out of her shock and stomped toward them.

A loud, angry growl filled the air. Juan's fist stopped midair, and they all turned to see Riel's pissed-off animal and Mr. Carson standing next to the wolf. She recognized Ry's animal instantly. Juan let go of her and she dragged herself along the long table away from him.

"What is going on here?" Mr. Carson demanded to know.

The big brown wolf stepped closer until he was only a few feet from her. He licked her face, his wolf's way of saying *I'll take care of this.* He stalked slowly forward, head down, teeth bared.

Sam watched as Riel lifted his nose and sniffed. He shifted and pointed to the cabinets below the coffee bar Juan stood in front of. Ry said, "Open that door." Whether from Ry's alpha command or curiosity, Juan did as told.

Sam couldn't see what was there since Ry stood between her and Juan.

Before she knew what was happening, Riel flew through the air toward her.

"Bomb!"

Sam felt the air pressure in the room change and a heavy weight on her before everything went black.

THIRTY-ONE

Riel felt shockwaves pass through him then heat burned his bare back, but he didn't move from where he covered his little mate's body with his. His ears rang even though the room was deathly silent except for wood and wall debris hitting the floor from being launched into the air.

After a few breaths, he lifted his head to look around. Sunshine beamed through the area where the wall used to be. The scent of blood reached his nose. Someone was hurt. He rolled off Sam and searched her for injuries. The blood wasn't hers.

Sam groaned and raised a hand to her head. "What happened? Why is my head pounding?"

He leaned down and brushed hair out of her face. "A bomb exploded."

She bolted up. "What? Oh my god." She

gazed around, making sense of the scene. More moans came from the back of the room. "Go help them, please. I'm fine."

Riel kissed her forehead and went in search of the others. The first person he came upon was Carson. The man rolled onto his side and pushed up.

He raised an arm. "Check the women. I'm all right."

The room stunk of ash and burnt flesh. The aunts had been pushed against the wall. Being that they were close to Carson, the blast wave hadn't harmed them except for a few scratches.

One of the aunts tried to stand. "Cece! Where's Cece?" Her legs being wobbly, Riel helped her back to the floor.

"I'll look for her. Stay here," he said. He remembered one of the aunts standing much closer to Juan. Glancing across the room, he guessed the older woman had to be buried under the pile of collapsed ceiling and wall.

Borrowing from his wolf, Riel hefted the conference table-topping the stack. In the distance, sirens whirred, getting louder every second. Thank goodness someone dialed 911. No one in the room had sense enough yet. When he pulled back a piece of drywall, a hand with manicured nails lay motionless. From there, Riel unburied the aunt then felt for a pulse.

He heard her heartbeat, but it wasn't a normal rhythm. The woman could be in the throes of a heart attack or worse. Earlier, he had performed CPR on his mate. He hoped he didn't have to do it again. Sam's aunt looked frail and he was afraid he'd break her ribs.

Suddenly, the woman sucked in a deep breath, but remained unconscious. Her heart returned to a steady beat. Riel lifted her fragile frame and made his way out the damaged door. He laid her on the sofa in the lobby.

First responders came through the front glass doors and froze in their tracks when seeing him. What? He wasn't injured. Then he watched as the firemen's eyes traveled down his body.

Oh fuck. He was naked from his emergency shift when Juan was hurting his mate. He snatched up a throw pillow on the sofa and covered his bits, large bits. Two medics came over to Sam's aunt. "She's stable now but may have had a heart issue before I got to her."

He hurried out to his truck for his stash of clothing he kept in the back. A couple of fire trucks took up most of the small lot. Ambulances screeched up the street. And a police car pulled up.

He traipsed back to the room, guiding the

other firemen, not that they could miss the site. Sam stood, staring at something at her feet. From behind, he wrapped his arms around her and looked over her shoulder.

On the floor, an arm with burned flesh and shredded suit coat sleeve lay. "I guess we don't have to worry about Juan anymore," she said with a sad sigh.

For the next hour, Riel and Sam helped their aunts to the ambulance for them to be checked out. Aunt Cece was taken to the hospital. Riel and Sam declined medical attention wanting to get home. After speaking with police, they were released only to bump into their alpha standing with the crowd, watching the event.

Chase frowned, concern on his face. "Both of you to my house. I want to be debriefed."

Riel groaned then settled his mate in his truck before climbing behind the wheel.

"I don't suppose we can pretend we didn't see him and go home?" Sam said.

He sighed. "Anyone except the alpha, yeah."

"That's what I thought."

Both remained quiet on the drive to Chase and Sophia's home. He'd have to give his mate extra attention tonight.

* * *

"Geez, your poor face. Does it hurt a lot?" Sophia asked.

Sam tried to ignore the burning and throbbing taking hold of her face. "Maybe a little," she lied.

Sophia smiled sympathetically and pointed to her nose. "Shifter, remember? You don't need to lie to me, Sam. I can get you something for the pain. Doc Raven always leaves me with supplies in case anyone comes over injured."

Sam noticed Chase was no longer in the kitchen, and wondered if he'd gone somewhere with Riel. Sophia guided her to one of the ground-level bedrooms. "Don't worry. Ry will know where you are and come for you in a moment. Let's get your face cleaned up so he doesn't get any more worried."

Sitting on the bed, Sam thought back through the chaotic event and wondered what the hell had gotten into Juan. She knew he had a short temper. It just went to prove that she was right, and he had more than anger problems. He had violent tendencies up the kazoo.

She flinched when Sophia used an alcohol pad to wipe at her cuts. Yeah. Juan the asshole deserved what he got, and Sam didn't feel a shred of sorrow for the jerk.

After Sophia cleaned Sam's face and had given her a mild painkiller, she told her to remove the scent of Juan in the attached bathroom.

She showered, and when she came out, she found shorts and a tank top that must've belonged to her new friend. The fit was perfect. She sat on the bed waiting for Riel to show. Countless minutes later, the door opened and Riel walked in wearing a pair of shorts and a T-shirt. He was clean and had clearly showered as well.

She stood and ran into his arms. It didn't matter that he was uncomfortable with her seeing him threatening to kill. He'd done it for her.

His voice was a deep growl when he spoke. "I'm sorry you had to see that."

"I'm not." She grabbed his face in her hands. "You saved me…again. He hurt me, and you stopped him. I could see the intent to continue hurting me. I can't begin thank you for what you did." She pulled his head down, kissed him, and ignored the stab of pain in her jaw.

He wrapped his hands around her waist and lifted her up to him. He rained soft kisses over her broken lips and spoke between kisses. "Sweetheart, I never wanted you to see that."

She tried to pacify him. "It doesn't matter, Ry. You're a shifter; it's who you are. I can't, nor would I want to, change that. I love you, animal, man, mate. I knew a relationship between us wouldn't be the usual human kind, and guess what? I wouldn't have it any other way."

"Sam—"

She placed a hand over his lips. "Stop, Ry. This is us. Our life. You can't honestly believe that you'd keep me in the dark forever. I love you, every single aspect of you. And I don't want you to ever hold back from being yourself because you're concerned over my reaction.

"Besides, when we have kids, they might come out with your traits and what are you going to do then?" She smiled when the mention of children brought a possessive grin to his face. "You know the chances are high that we will have shifter babies, so just get over it."

She sniffed his neck and felt his cock harden and rub against her belly. Her sex turned slick instantly. "Let's go home."

He growled softly. "Sounds like a fantastic idea to me." He grabbed her by her ass cheeks, rocked her over his cock, and groaned.

She laughed. "Are we going home or what?" Lust made the beating of her heart frantic.

"In a minute." He slipped his hands under her tank top and palmed her breasts. She moaned and licked his neck.

To her thinking, a minute wasn't such a bad idea. She stripped off her clothes and dropped down to her knees, then jerked down his pants. Licking her lips, she watched his cock spring free, thick, aroused, and so purple, she swore all his blood was centered in his shaft. She was about to suck him into her mouth, but her jaw burned at the attempt to widen her lips.

He must've seen her flinch, because he pulled her up by her shoulders. "As much as I love your lips on me, I don't want you to do it when you're not well. You're in pain."

She pouted and winced.

"Another time, my love." He kissed her softly and growled into her lips.

She jerked his cock in her hand.

He hissed out a groan. "Jesus, you're going to be the death of me."

"Only if we go there together." She sat back on the bed, crawled backward until she was lying in the middle of the mattress, and opened her thighs wide. She slid her hand between her legs and fingered herself.

Wet heat dripped from her slit. Desire flared brightly in her veins, pushing her to act. She caressed her chest and pinched at a nipple with her other hand. Fire shot through her pussy and made her womb clench. His nose flared, and he licked his lips as if he could already taste her. The thought made a crazy gallop take over her chest.

"Sam…you're playing with fire."

"Good. Because I want you to brand me, take me, and fuck me right now. I'm yours. Now get over here and do me before I lose my mind." She widened her eyes at the aggression rushing through her. There was no helping it. He was hers, and she wanted him now. Right now.

He laughed and removed the rest of his clothes. "I always knew you were a bossy little minx. Good thing I'm such a patient, loving man," he joked and jumped on the bed. He sniffed her from ankle to her dripping sex.

She widened her thighs. "Yes! Please, please, please."

He blew cool air over her clit, and she almost came off the bed. She glanced down to catch him grinning at her. "What do you want, Sam?" The deep voice made her pussy throb in need.

She growled and lifted her ass off the bed and brought her clit right to his lips. "I want you to eat my pussy and make me come. Is that clear enough for you?"

He growled and licked a slow trail up her pussy lips. "Oh, yeah. I love it when you talk dirty to me."

She groaned a laugh. He was going to drive

her insane. He trailed a wet finger into her anal entrance, sucked down on her clit, and grazed his teeth over her swollen nub.

Her climax slammed into her like a Mack truck. She came so hard, she dug her nails into the comforter in a white-knuckle grip, her body spasming and legs shaking. Her pussy clenched on air, and she whimpered at the empty feeling inside.

She pulled at his short hair. His hot body caressed her flesh on his way up. He took her, filling her, making her nerves tingle and her breath hitch.

Each thrust into her pussy had her grasping and reaching for the pleasure she knew was just a little further. He continued to thrust repeatedly and she moaned, her insides burning with arousal. He flicked a finger over her clit, and she shattered.

He brought his head down and kissed her, drinking in her scream. As she panted, he growled into her neck, and his cock jerked inside her hot channel. He came in long shudders, snarled, and dropped to the bed. He pulled her up until she lay draped over him like a blanket. "Okay. We can go home now."

She lifted her head from his chest. "I think I need another minute."

THIRTY-TWO

Sam was positive that Juan Junior had been her threat until the bomb exploded. All her aunts were there, so the stalker was someone else completely. Now she was thoroughly confused.

All along, she'd thought it was about her inheritance and dying within thirty days. But, again, everyone in the will was in the room. Why else would someone want to hurt her?

She asked Riel, "What are you thinking?"

"We still don't know what's going on with Danitelli. Someone was working with a woman. I keep getting a sweet scent every time something happens to you." Riel sounded puzzled. She hadn't thought about spouses. None were at the meeting.

Her eyes widened. "Marcia? But she's the mousiest woman ever. I don't see that in her."

He clenched his jaw and shook his head. "I've seen her; I don't think she was part of the threat either. I don't know what's going on, but there's something we're not seeing."

"Who else could there be? My family is filled with snobs, but it isn't that big. Half the people don't even live in Black Meadows. The only ones left here are the older folks."

Riel glanced her way. "We're still searching into Luisa and Cecilia."

A shocked gasp left her. "Luisa? But she's not like the rest of them. She's sweet and kind, and Cecilia is not the nicest, but —" She wondered how her aunt was doing. She needed to visit her at the hospital. She'd get the hospital and room number from one of the other aunts.

"She's living with a young stud who she gives every cent to in order to keep him with her. She's completely broke and needs the money in order to entertain her young lover."

Her family definitely had drama. Still, Cecilia being with a younger man wasn't a crime. "So what's the big deal that she's giving her money to her younger lover?"

He glanced at her and grimaced. She knew she wasn't going to like what he said.

"That younger lover is sleeping with three other rich women, and he's an ex-con that was in prison for attempted murder and assault."

Oh damn. That didn't sound too promising for Cecilia. "Well, what's going on with Luisa? She's not like them; she's different. As for Cecilia, she's always been like Maggie, cold and living by society's rule book.

"Those women have been super strict as far as I can remember in trying to set the pace that everyone in society should follow. From their homes to how a woman needs to behave. Thank god neither of them ever had kids."

He nodded. "What can you tell me about their husbands?"

"Maggie went through four divorces before she met Danitelli. She's been with him for fifteen years, I think. I'm not sure what happened, but from what Ginny used to say, her previous husbands felt she was much too bossy for their tastes.

"Cecilia was married, and her husband was a general in the Army. I think I was fifteen when he left her for a young woman he met in Vietnam. Cecilia was hit hard.

"She'd always acted as if she had the perfect family. Ginny said if she'd paid more attention to what was going on inside the family instead of how the world perceived them, she might have seen that one coming."

"What can you tell me about Danitelli?"

"Ugh. Not much, unfortunately. He's always in some business or other, but he's never really bothered with our side of the family. He's from some big Italian family. I think they come from money, so I'm not sure what he would want with Ginny's money."

"It's five billion dollars. Anybody—even someone with money—would want to get their hands on that."

She sighed.

"What about Luisa?"

Sam sighed again. "She was married to a doctor for a long time. He was much older than her and died when I left for college. I think she loved him, because she stayed alone after that. I never heard of her being with anyone else. It was sad to see her so lonely.

"She's the only one of the three women that had kids. Two boys. I remember wishing she'd talk to me more, but she was always surrounded by the other two, and so I never tried to get close to her. Cecilia and Maggie were pretty mean, so I stayed away."

"Mean how?"

She leaned her head back in the seat. "They tended to mention what a shame my mother was to the family. Now I realize it wasn't only the shifter friends they were against, it was my father. Mom's relationship with him had drawn bad blood from the others."

They turned onto his street, and she caught sight of Nat in front of his house. He parked the truck at the curb and turned to her. He cupped her cheek and stared at her intently.

"We are still investigating Luisa. I can't say for sure that she's out of the picture until I hear back from Kane. And I'm not sure what Kane has on Danitelli, so we're still on the lookout.

"So far, I know there was a woman involved in the attempts on your life, and I'm not going to let this go until I know who it was. All I ask is that you're careful. I'm not happy with this, and I have a feeling we're missing something."

She kissed him then jumped out of the SUV and headed to the front of the house. Nat had a bakery box in her hand wrapped with a pink-and-gold ribbon. She knew the local bakery. It was really popular, and their sweets were out of this world.

Her mouth watered just thinking of whatever was inside the box. The craving for chocolate had been at her for two days, and she'd been ignoring it, but now that she thought of the decadent sweets, she almost drooled. "Please tell me that there's chocolate in there." She smiled hopefully.

Nat grinned and passed her the cake box. "I wanted to bring you something special to welcome you back to health. Yes, it is chocolate. Actually, it's Tryx's famous chocolate mousse cake. I called your cell phone, but I didn't get you." She frowned as she neared Sam. "What the hell happened to you?"

After she'd taken the medication for the pain she'd forgotten about the small cuts and bruises. "Juan Junior." She was too exhausted to go into the bomb details. She'd mention it tomorrow when her mind was clear.

Nat slapped her hands on her hips and huffed. "I knew that piece of crap was going to be trouble. What did he do?"

Sam glanced at Riel. "Do you mind checking to see if I left my phone upstairs? If I didn't, then that means it's back at Sophia's, and I'll need a way to get it back." She hoped he'd go for the request. When he nodded, she sighed in relief. She didn't want to discuss what happened in front of him.

He rushed up the stairs as she headed to the kitchen with Nat. She grabbed a knife, plates, and forks for the cake. Nat set the coffee

qmaker to brew.

"So?" Nat's voice was filled with curiosity.

She placed the cake box on the table and

opened it. "He started talking trash about my parents."

Sam lifted the cake, and Nat removed the box. "What kind of trash did he talk? I mean what did he say to make things get that bad?"

Sam cut a large piece of cake, placed it on a plate, and stared at it. She then cut another piece and added it to the first one. "He said my mother was a whore because she'd fallen in love with my father, who was a shifter and one of Chase's father's enforcers."

She moved the plate to the side. When Nat tried to grab it, she smacked her hand away. "That one is mine."

Nat gaped at her with wide eyes. "Okay, okay. I'll take the next piece. Sheesh." She stuck her tongue out. "Anyway, tell me more about this. Your father was a shifter? Oh my god. That's huge." She bounced on the chair. "But why don't you shift?"

She cut a much smaller piece of cake. Her best friend studied the plate, glanced at her, and raised her brows. Nat's loud sigh said she knew Sam wasn't trying to share.

Sam sat and inhaled the delicious scent of chocolate, milk, and sugar. "I'm not sure why I am not a shifter, but Sophia is checking out my blood. Apparently, it could be anything that caused me not to be one of them." She bit into the cake and moaned.

Nat laughed. Sam opened her eyes to catch her grinning.

"I knew you'd love it. Tryx's chocolate cake seems to be a favorite among shifters and humans. Although from what I've heard, pregnant shifters crave it like a drug."

Sam stopped the fork midway to her mouth. She glanced at Nat's smirk and shook her head. "You fantasize too much. Just for that, you don't get any more of my cake."

Nat waved the chocolate-covered fork in the air. "So what exactly did Juan do?"

She licked the fork and took another bite. "He started talking smack, and I got fed up. I yelled and told him the entire estate is going to charity. He went berserk. Slapped me multiple times. I tried to get away, but he had a tight grip on my shirt."

Nat stopped eating. "What happened then?"

"Ry showed up. Juan dropped me." She remembered how angry he'd been.

Nat sat unmoving. "Wow."

She shoved a big bite of cake into her mouth and moaned. "Mmm. I know. God this cake is fantastic. Do you think she puts something special in here? I've made cake tons of times, and they never tasted this good! I want to buy her to make this for me every day."

"It's from an old family recipe, but we can make arrangements for you to get as much of it as you want." Riel's deep voice made her and Nat both turn to face him. He stood by the kitchen door.

He crossed the room and poured coffee. He silently offered her a cup and she shook her head in a negative. All she wanted was cake. He grinned, and she wondered what he found amusing.

He sat in the chair next to her and used his thumb to clean off the chocolate frosting from the corner of her mouth. "It's supposed to go in your mouth, not on it." Her throat dried when he sucked the thumb into his own mouth.

Nat sighed a complaint. "Oh, brother. Can you hold off all that private couple stuff until I'm gone? I don't want to leave here needing therapy...or to get laid."

They continued to chat until Nat had to leave. Nat bounced toward her friend and gave her a hug. "Okay, I'm going." She grinned and glanced at the cake. "Try not to eat that in one sitting. I have a feeling you're going to need more of it."

Nat left. Sam jumped when her stomach growled. What the hell? She looked down at her empty plate and then up at Riel. He watched her with raised brows.

"What?" She stood. "This is what happens when you don't feed me. I'm going to make a sandwich, or two." Or three. She strolled toward the fridge, stopped and turned to glance back at Riel. He was still watching her. "Don't touch my cake!" She marched in search of food, lots of it.

THIRTY-THREE

Sam opened her eyes and groaned. She was starving but so damn tired. It was probably from all the craziness of the past few weeks. Her body was finally giving out on her. She sat up on the bed and groaned at the cramping in her stomach. Riel's footsteps sounded, rushing down the hallway until his body filled the doorway.

"What's wrong, sweetheart?" He walked into the room and stopped next to the bed.

She dropped back into the pillows with a groan. "I'm either starving to death or dying from exhaustion and starving at the same time."

"What?" He frowned as if she'd been speaking in another language.

She groaned through the hair that covered her face. "Food. I need food and sleep. God, I'm tired. I think all my running around has finally caught up with me."

He pushed the curls away from her face. She glanced up into his worried eyes. "I'll get you some food, you get some sleep. You're sure that's all? Are you in any other kind of pain?"

She shook her head. "No, just hungry. Well…more like starving."

He nodded and turned to the door. "All right. I'll be right back."

Good, because she didn't think she'd make it out of bed. She was exhausted. Falling into a fitful sleep, she groaned again at the sharp cramps hitting her stomach. When the smell of food reached her, she sat up in a flash.

Riel walked in carrying a tray brimming with food. She checked herself for drool. It would be such a shame for her man to see that this early in their relationship. He put the tray on the bed. He'd made her steak and eggs. How did he know she loved that? She grabbed the plate and a fork, cutting a nice chunk of meat and shoving it into her mouth. It was absolutely delicious. So much so, she moaned as she chewed.

"Thank you," she said through bites. It alarmed her a little when she ate the contents on the plate and was still hungry.

She glanced at him, wondering what he'd think, but he just grabbed a second plate and passed it to her. That plate had buttered toast, an omelet, and home fries. Digging into the food, she wondered if she had been eating too little lately.

She'd never had problems eating, but the last few weeks were one big, jumbled mess in her mind. She was sure she'd never finish everything on the plate. It was a good thing she didn't voice her opinion. Not ten minutes later she was passing him an empty plate. What the hell was wrong with her? Had her body finally decided it needed more food to sustain her curves?

Riel didn't seem bothered by her overeating. In fact, he smiled wide and passed more food her way. When he offered her a cup with coffee and a glass of juice, she wrinkled her nose at the coffee and grabbed the juice instead. That's when exhaustion hit full force. She leaned back and shut her eyes.

When Sam woke again, she was alone in the bedroom. Moonlight filtered through the windows. Damn, how long had she slept? She stood and sniffed. Moisture gathered in her mouth. Burgers. Yum.

Before slipping on her shoes, she put on a pair of shorts and a tank top. When she reached the bottom of the stairs, she heard Ry talking to Troy in the backyard. There was no longer a need to question how she could hear them from so far away.

Troy's voice sounded surprised. "You're sure?"

Ry's sighed. "No, I'm not sure. It's the same thing Sophia experienced. Not to the degree she had it, but the exhaustion and the hunger. It's all there. Not to mention she smells different, but I can't tell this soon. Only Chase, Tryx, and now Sophia have that keen a sense." Ry's deep voice seeped into her pores and made warmth spread through her. Was he talking about her?

"I guess I should congratulate you then." Congratulate him? About what?

"Not until we know for sure. I'll have to take her over to Chase and Sophia's for blood testing." What test? Frustration started to mount. She wanted them to speak clearer so she could understand what they were referring to.

"Wow. But if you're right then that means she's pregnant." Troy's excitement made her excited too. Until she replayed his words and inhaled sharply.

Oh my god. Her hands flew to her stomach. Was she pregnant? Was that the reason she'd been starving?

She was about to head to the kitchen when a soft knock sounded at the front door. She pulled the door open. Shock made her stand there for a moment, unable to move. Her aunt Luisa was at the door. Her heart immediately went out to the soft-spoken woman.

"Aunt Luisa, what are you doing here? What's wrong?"

"It's Cece. Maggie said she's dying and to come get you. We need to get to the hospital right away." Her aunt broke down in tears. Sam put her arms around her feeble aunt and guided her to the driver's door of the woman's car. "Oh, dear," she said, "will you drive. I can't see through my tears."

Sam's brows lifted, but what the hell? "Sure, Aunt Luisa. I just need to let Riel know where I'm going."

"No," her aunt said. "There's no time for that. We have to go *now*." The vehemence in her voice startled Sam. They reversed direction and walked around the car. After getting the older lady buckled in, Sam climbed in. She'd call Riel from the hospital. He'd probably not even know she left.

Luisa glanced at Sam and made a sad attempt to smile through her tears. Poor woman. She was so distressed, Sam's first instinct was to make her feel better. Sam started the engine and pulled into the street. There were two hospitals in town, both on the east side.

"What all did Maggie say about Aunt

Cecilia?" Sam asked.

Luisa dabbed at her nose. "Just that she was bad and needed us."

That seemed a little strange. As far as she knew, Cece and the others didn't give a shit about her, much less needed her. Luisa bawled louder.

She patted the older woman on her arm. "Are you going to be okay?"

Luisa blew her nose. "It's just that I need to beg you to help me. I never thought I'd have to do this, but with Mother leaving you her estate, I find myself without anyone to ask for assistance."

Her heart broke for her poor aunt. She knew the others usually pushed her around. "Of course. Whatever you need, tell me."

Luisa's shaky hand reached into her large handbag for what she assumed was a tissue to clear away the tears. What she pulled out was no tissue. Her dear old aunt held a Magnum .357 in a very steady grip.

Luisa shook her head. "Sam, I'm sorry." She kept her voice soft. "I really am, but I need you to die." She cocked the gun to prove she meant business.

Sam stared in shock at the woman then at the road. Her brain refused to accept what she saw. This made no sense. Then it did. This wasn't about Aunt Cecilia.

Sam wanted to kick her own ass for being such a fool. She should've listened to Ry when he told her things were still unsettled. She gulped and thought of what Troy had said. She might be pregnant and had now placed her child in danger. "Luisa, what are you doing?"

With Sam in the driver's seat, Luisa pushed the gun into Sam's head.

Luisa smirked, and Sam started to panic. "I know all about the shifter-enhanced hearing. Trust me, your mother told me things."

"How did you know I'd get the door?"

Luisa rolled her eyes. "You have huge bay windows with no curtains, incredibly tacky and stupid at the same time. I saw you walking down the stairs. I'd seen the men heading for the backyard earlier."

Sam tried to think of a way to get out of the situation without getting herself killed. "What exactly do you want, Luisa?"

"I want the money that belongs to me." Luisa's voice rose the farther away they drove.

Sam shook her head in confusion. "But Ginny left you a million dollars, Luisa. I know you don't live with high expenses, so why do you need more money?"

"Because my sons are sick." Luisa's voice lowered again with each word.

Sam had never heard of Luisa's kids being sick. She'd always boasted of them working for international companies and traveling the world in their successful careers. "Sick how?"

Luisa's sadness still made her feel bad for the woman. She looked a lot like Sam's mother. "My oldest has a small drug problem. He tends to spend all our money on the stuff and needs help."

Sam grimaced. "If he's spending all your money, what he needs is rehab."

"Don't you think I know that?!" Luisa shrieked.

Shit. She'd pissed her off. Sam had been slowing down in the hopes that Luisa hadn't noticed. They weren't too far from the house, but the area was still somewhat deserted. Riel's and Sam's houses had been located in a section where there was a lot of space between neighbors. She tried to keep Luisa talking. "What's wrong with your other son?"

"He's a bit of a compulsive gambler." When Sam made a face to match her distaste, her aunt rushed on. "But he's going to get help. He's just always waiting for the big win, and I don't have the money to wait on him anymore."

Wow. The entire family had treated Sam like a piece of trash because one of her parents had been a shifter, and all along they should've focused on their own issues.

She continued driving straight instead of taking a curved road that would lead her to the highway. By going straight, they were forced to stop when they reached a dead end.

"Why are you stopping?" Luisa demanded, not taking her eyes off Sam's face.

Sam turned to Luisa. "We're at a dead end."

Luisa peered around and lowered the gun to shove it into Sam's side. "I guess this spot can work just as well. Get out of the car."

Sam had to do something before things went downhill for her. She half turned toward the door handle, felt Luisa move closer to her, and slammed her elbow back into Luisa's face.

"You bitch!" Luisa screamed.

Sam reached for the hand holding the gun.

Blood covered the older woman's face, but Sam was focused on fighting her for the weapon. She'd never have guessed Luisa had such a strong grip. Sam struggled to get the gun from Luisa and keep it from pointing in her own direction at the same time.

A shot rang out inside the car, and she heard glass breaking. There was no time to talk or try to convince her aunt to stop. This was a fight for survival. She managed to turn the muzzle enough so the gun now pointed in Luisa's direction.

Luisa screeched and fought her for the gun. "Let go. I'm going to kill you for this."

Sam tried really hard not to lose her grip on the gun that was facing away from her. "Luisa, don't do anything stupid. This can be worked out." She continued to try to pull the weapon from the other woman.

"Are you kidding? Juan Junior said he'd take care of you, but what good was he? He sent you a bomb, and nothing. We sat in the car, watched you reach for the package. We had to leave before we could figure out if it had killed you, only to find out later that you were alive!"

She screamed through the tugging. "You were supposed to die when we lit your house on fire, and yet you're still here! Now, I have to do this myself. You are just like your mother, consorting with animals," Luisa spat in disgust.

That did it. Her emotions raged, and she turned the gun fully on Luisa. Luisa screamed as the bones in her hands popped, and she squeezed the trigger involuntarily.

Sam knew that shot had hit the mark. Luisa stopped struggling and glanced down at her chest. A small, red dot spread over the pristine silk blouse until the white material was covered in red. The raven-haired woman fell back into her seat, eyes open and mouth agape.

The driver-side door was torn from the hinges, making Sam scream in fear. Riel's angry, panting face scanned down her body.

She shook her head. "I'm fine." The finality of the situation got to her, and she threw her arms around his neck and started sobbing.

Riel's hold on her tightened. "I've got you."

She nodded into his shoulder through her tears. "I know."

THIRTY-FOUR

A couple days after the last attempt on Sam's life, the group gathered in Riel's living room.

"Okay, Sam," Sophia said, "I've got your test results. But before we get to it, explain to me how you guys know it was only Luisa and Juan Junior and not Danitelli or one of the others."

Riel spoke up. "Luisa told Sam all the attempts on her life had come from her and Juan Junior."

"But what about Danitelli?" Sophia asked.

"We found out that while he does have some weird ties to the mob, he wasn't involved in any of Sam's death threats. He's been taking over his sick uncle's business, and it's why he's been so hard to trace. But he didn't really have anything to show him as a culprit."

"What about the aunts?" Nat asked.

"Oh. Well, you all know Cecilia is paying off the younger man to be with her, but she recently found out he was cheating with some other women and dumped him."

Sam was glad her aunt Cece was released from the hospital and had returned home. But knowing she was alone worried her. No matter how mean the aunt was, she was still family.

Riel continued. "As for Maggie, she's busy being the new matriarch in Danitelli's family. Juan Senior is still in the Philippines, and Luisa's two sons are overseas hiding from drug and gambling debts."

"Could they come and do something to Sam?" Kane asked.

"We've got some of our friends in the London pack keeping tabs on them. We'll know if they try anything," Chase added. He glanced at Sophia and then at Sam. "All right, love. I think if you don't tell Sam her test results, she's going to have a mild panic attack soon." He grinned.

Sam's leg shook from nerves. Riel must've noticed her anxiety because he picked her up from her seat and set her in his lap. The move instantly calmed her. She curled her arms around his neck and turned to Sophia. "Okay. So what did you find out?"

Sophia grimaced. "I'm sorry, Sam. I have two theories. It is possible that your mother had a gene which kept her from turning shifter when she mated and that gene was passed on to you."

"There's no way to tell?"

"No. I would need your mother's DNA to test to see if it was a genetic anomaly. My other theory is that her treatment with those drugs killed any chances for you to be a shifter. The compounds were super strong. I'm surprised they didn't kill you in her womb."

Sam wasn't surprised. She'd had a feeling from what she'd read that the drugs had caused her to be in her current state. Too bad she'd never be a shifter.

"But I do have good news." Sophia smiled. "What?" All Sophia was supposed to look for was the alteration to her DNA.

Sophia sat on Chase's lap and grinned at them. "You're going to have a baby."

A chorus of "what" and "congratulations" sounded in the room.

"Hold on a second," Sam interjected, confused as hell that Sophia could know something that soon. "How can you tell when it can't be more than a week or two?"

Everyone laughed.

Sophia winked at her. "Well...shifter babies develop a lot faster than a human baby. What would be a nine-month pregnancy with a human is a six-month pregnancy with a shifter."

She gulped, unsure how to handle the whole going-to-be-a-mother thing so soon.

"And," Sophia continued over the loud voices, "I don't think the problem with the lacking gene will pass on to your offspring. Your baby should be full-blown shifter." She grinned and pointed at her own nose. "This little baby doesn't lie. I can smell the tiny wolf a mile away."

Riel turned Sam in his lap and grabbed her face in his hands. He kissed her so softly she forgot all about how Sophia knew she was pregnant. She became oblivious to their audience until someone cleared their throat.

"Um, excuse me," Nat broke in. "But I'd like to hug the mom-to-be sometime before the baby is born. And I'm not trying to see any adult-rated shows anytime soon," she complained.

"Come on, Nat. I can show you some great sights in private," Kane quipped.

"Over my dead body," Troy growled.

She lifted her face to her mate's. The look of total adoration in his eyes made her heart flip. She turned to Nat who sat between Troy and Kane. They were ready to fight for the rights to her best friend. It was funny to see and so obvious to her that Kane was only trying to rile up Troy.

Sam stood and was enveloped in multiple hugs until she found herself being pulled to the kitchen by Sophia's sister, Julia, and Nat.

Sam's smile grew when she noticed what was on the kitchen table. The women turned to Nat, and she grinned. "I know how you pregnant shifters or almost shifters get without your chocolate, so I begged Tryx to hook you guys up. One for each, so there's no fighting."

Julia stopped in her tracks. "Oh god. Is that—"

Sophia bounced toward the table. "Yes! You sneaked these past us? How did you know we'd love this, Nat?"

Nat laughed. "I don't know, but from what I saw of Sam, you guys have a sweet tooth that can't be cured." She grinned. "And really, who the hell doesn't love chocolate cake? That's just insanity."

When the women pointed at the two cakes, she smirked. "You girls don't think the guys and I deserve a piece?"

They all laughed.

Sam had to hand it to Nat. She fit right in with the shifter group. They each cut a large piece and walked out to the yard where the new nurse guarded over Shane and Selena. Riel walked up behind her and wrapped his arms around her waist. She sighed and leaned back into him.

He fluttered his lips over her ear. "Thank you," he whispered.

She lifted her head and peered at his beautiful golden eyes. "For what?"

He turned her in his arms. Her breath hitched at the emotion in his eyes. "For coming home."

She pulled his head down for a kiss. Ginny's death might have brought her home, but her mate was the reason she stayed.

Chase's phone rang. She tried not to listen in, like everyone else, but with their super hearing, that was almost impossible.

She didn't know the voice on the phone, but it seemed Ry did. His body stiffened at the first words. Something was going on—a fight maybe—and it had gotten bloody.

Chase hung up and glanced at the guys—his enforcers—standing around. Ry kissed her then looked into her eyes. "We'll be back shortly. You and the girls hang out and eat."

She snorted at him. Just because she was pregnant didn't mean—well, okay. Yes, it did. She'd eat anything put in front of her.

The guys headed out and the women looked at each other. "Anyone for more cake?" They all rushed into the kitchen.

Sam caught a glimpse of the packet her grandmother's will was in. She'd brought it to the house with the small chest before the fire. Ry must've left it on the counter after he took the chest to the bedroom. She grabbed it and sat at the table.

"What's that?" Nat asked as she dished out more cake. The others took seats around the table.

"It's a copy of my grandmother's last will and testament. I wanted to read through it to see what it says." She flipped through the pages to the location where the estate was dispersed. The girls kept chatting, adding ease to the kitchen.

Sam's eyes skimmed the words that said if she'd died in the next thirty days, the money would go to her aunts and cousins and the charities in Section XI of the will.

Sam shuffled through the pages to Section XI. The first two charities she recognized the names. Her grandmother had supported them for years. The last one must've been a new organization as she'd never heard Grandmother talk about it. She'd ask Mr. Carson for details on it.

Shit. She really needed to sign whatever

papers Mr. Carson needed. She intended to stop by his office days ago and then all the attempts on her life started and the fire. She'd have to thank him for his patience.

She glanced at her watch. There were two hours before Juan Junior's funeral. After pulling her phone from her pocket, she dialed the lawyer's number. Mr. Carson said he'd be in his office for a while if she wanted to come in.

"Hey, y'all," Sam said, "I need to run to my lawyer's office for a minute. There's a few things to wrap up still."

Sophia chimed in, "Since the danger is over, this would be a good time with the guys busy."

"I'll probably be back before they return," Sam replied. She snatched up her purse, dropping her phone in and taking out her keys. She'd have to apologize profusely to Mr. Carson for dragging this out so long.

THIRTY-FIVE

Sam parked out front of the law offices of Carson & Willis. She sat in the car and stared at the weather-worn building. From this angle, she couldn't see any of the damage to the back of the building.

The paint was peeling from the siding. The front brick façade was cracked, and a few pieces lay on the ground, crumbled into smaller debris. The place didn't look kept up. Not what she expected.

Ginny had brought her here once when she was younger. This almost didn't look like the same location. But the sign read the attorney's name.

Gathering her purse, she got out of the car and crossed the pothole-filled lot. Inside, there was an empty desk in the front where a receptionist would normally sit. After the explosion, maybe they shut down most of the business. But Carson said to meet him here.

Not sure what to do or where to go, she called out. When she heard a familiar voice, she followed it to a hallway. Mr. Carson walked toward her, a bit slumped from age, she supposed.

"Sorry about no one being out here to greet you. Times being what they are, we had to let our receptionist go. Too much competition." He shook his head and turned down the hallway. When she was at the office the other day, she hadn't even noticed the desk was unoccupied. She had other things on her mind at the time.

Mr. Carson rounded the corner then opened a back door. Sam stopped. "Are the papers outside?"

Mr. Carson chuckled. "I apologize. Your grandmother has one last item for your eyes only. It's a bit of a drive to get there."

"Oh" was all she could say. With that, she walked out. He guided her to his car, opened the door for her and made sure she was tucked inside before closing the door.

She was surprised how old his car was. She thought lawyers had the big bucks. Business must be very slow.

He pulled out of the back parking lot and headed down the street. After a few minutes of silence, Sam asked, "What is this item Grandmother had?"

Mr. Carson glanced at her. "I don't know. It's for you only. I just have instructions on how to get there."

She turned to the window and watched the town zip by.

"You know, your grandmother missed you these past five years," he said. "She talked a lot about you and how proud she was of you."

She turned to him, tears in her eyes. "She was?"

"Oh, my, yes. Without you, she would've considered her life a failure."

"Why? She had tons of money. More than she could spend," she replied.

"Now, Samira, you know your beloved grandmother did not put faith into material objects."

Yes, she did know that. She was almost ashamed of what she said. "What was her failure then?"

Mr. Carson snorted. "Her children, of course. Not one of them is worth a grain of salt." He shook his head. "Have you found out who set the fire to the house?"

"Yes. Seems Juan Junior and Luisa were behind it all. They wanted the money they'd get if I died."

His shoulders slumped a bit. "I'm sorry about all that, Samira. Had I known how conniving and desperate Ginny's children were, I would not have read that line about you dying in the will. It was my fault."

"No, Mr. Carson, you couldn't have known how they would react. Granted, they act spoiled and like bratty children, but death threats? Even I didn't see that coming."

He said, "I agree on them acting spoiled, not to mention being morons. They can't do anything right, even paired up, obviously."

Had she heard that right? It sounded like he was disgusted with the siblings' failed attempts. He glanced at her, a frown on his face. The tension in the air grew thick.

Her phone rang in her purse. As she leaned forward, he put his arm out and pushed her back in the seat. "Do not answer that." An unusual look in his eyes frightened her. Her heart tumbled. What was going on?

THIRTY-SIX

Riel got out of Chase's vehicle, opening and closing his fist.

"You know, Riel," Chase said, "you didn't have to knock out the guy. We could've just tackled him and shoved his face into the ground."

"Sorry," Riel replied, "I didn't mean to take away all your fun. I wanted to get back as soon as possible. Watching you play with your food isn't on my to-do list."

Riel looked around and didn't see Sam's car. God damn it. Did she go off without him again?

"Chill out, Riel," Chase said, "she'll be fine. The two trying to kill her are dead."

He stopped in his tracks and glared at the alpha. "How do you what I'm thinking?"

Chase grunted. "I have a mate who is like

Sam. She doesn't heed what I say any more than yours. Especially when I tell her not to do something."

"Are mates always this nerve-racking?" Riel asked.

"Yup, get used to it. I wouldn't have it any other way."

Riel smiled. He wouldn't want it any other way either. He'd take Sam unconditionally.

The guys filed through the door to see the women gathered around the kitchen table.

Sophia saw them first. "Hey. That was fast. What happened?"

Chase rounded the table and laid a long kiss on his mate. Jealousy rose in Riel, wanting to do the same to his mate. Of course, she wasn't at the table.

"Um," he started, "did Sam say where she was going and when she'd be back?"

Nat glanced at the clock over the sink. "She went to sign something at her lawyer's. She said she'd be right back and that was thirty minutes ago."

Riel read the worry on Nat's face. He went into the other room and dialed her number. As he waited, Riel became more freaked out with each ring. Why wasn't she picking up? Frustrated, he hung up and walked into the kitchen.

He glanced at the stack of papers in front of an empty chair. His eyes scanned the page, picking up the family names and then a line that stopped his breathing.

Riel read the line three times. No wonder Sam's aunts and cousin wanted her dead. And as far as he was concerned, until those thirty days passed, his mate was in danger.

Out of curiosity, he flipped through the will paperwork to Section XI to see what charities Ginny cared for the most. The first two she talked about all the time, but the third, he'd never heard.

He pulled his phone from his pocket and googled Sisterhood of the Assembly. That was strange. They had no website, no news article, no fake news. Nothing.

He asked the ladies. "If a charity doesn't have a website and their name doesn't come up anywhere, what would you think?"

"I'd think they were a secret organization or didn't exist," Sophia said.

Nat added, "Everybody has a website, no matter how small they are."

A chill ran up his spine. He dialed her again, and again, it went to voicemail. His fist hit the table, startling everyone.

"I'm going to that lawyer's office ," he said. "Something's wrong."

"Want me to go with you?" Chase asked.

"Nah, I just need to talk to Sam. She's not answering her phone."

With shifter speed, he was in his truck and had it in gear within record time. Speeding and going through an orange stop light, he turned the corner to see the small building and a tow truck hooking up to Sam's car.

"What the fuck?"

Riel jumped the curb and raced into the parking lot. Barely stopped, he was out and in the tow truck driver's face.

"Why are you taking this car?" Riel asked. The heavily tattooed man pointed a meaty finger toward the front door. Riel kept his eyes on the man. "This car belongs to a woman inside. She needs it to drive home. Unhook it."

The hulking man crossed his arms over his extended belly. "No can do, buddy. The owners of this lot called to have this car taken away. I'm just doing my job."

Riel stuck a finger in the guy's face. "Wait till I get back. Stay here." He spun on his heel toward the building's glass-door entrance. He saw a man in a suit standing on the other side of the door. When the man saw him stomping in his direction, the little shit locked the door. That did not sit well with Riel.

Riel pounded his fist on the glass, causing the guy to step back farther. "Hey," Riel said, "Sam Suarez is here. She's my fiancée." Not totally the truth, but that's how he considered it. She was marrying him no matter what. "I need to talk to her."

The guy yelled, "She's not here. She left." He then scuttled across the lobby and down the hall.

Motherfucker. In seconds, his elbow was through the glass and it crumbled around him as he stepped inside.

He heard an interior door slam and nearly laughed. A piece of wood wasn't stopping him from finding out where his mate was. He passed the destroyed conference room, listening for the single heartbeat in the building. One shoulder slam and the entire side of the door frame shattered into splinters.

Riel had the man by the throat and smashed against the wall before the guy finished dialing his phone.

"Where is she?"

The attorney's face paled and his eyes bugged completely out. He shook his head and tried to talk. Riel realized he'd have to let up for the man to be able to speak, but that didn't make his wolf happy. His hand loosened. "Talk."

"She left with Carson," the guy said.

"Where?" Riel demanded.

The lawyer's head shook again. "I don't know. He didn't tell me. I just saw them walk out."

Riel dropped the guy and rushed down the hall, looking for an exit. Following the sign attached to the ceiling tile, he turned the corner and was rewarded with his objective.

Slamming the door open to crash into the wall, he took a deep breath. Sam's scent registered, but it was faint. She had been here. But where was she now?

He ran the path he'd come and stepped through the shattered entrance. The tow truck driver and Sam's car were gone. Fuck! But another truck he knew pulled up.

Chase and the other guys piled out. "Riel," Chase said, concern burning in his eyes, "what's going on?"

Riel paced, shoving a hand through his hair. "I'm not sure, but I think Sam's in trouble."

"Why?" Chase answered. Riel quickly explained his suspicions based on the will, unknown charity, and Sam being gone. Then he realized why the tow truck was taking her car;

Sam wasn't supposed to come back. They were hiding evidence she was ever there.

Fuck! Fuck! Fuck! His wolf perched just under his skin, wanting out to find their mate. But she was in a damn car. There was no scent to follow.

Chase tapped his phone. "Let me see where Soph is. She was following us but got stuck by the train."

Riel watched his alpha bring up an app displaying the town and a flashing blue dot. Then it hit him. Riel had downloaded the same app to his and Sam's phones some time ago. He was cooking and had her phone. He'd set it on the counter when she came down the stairs.

With shaking hands, he pulled out his phone. Twice, he mis-typed the passcode and was ready to throw the piece of shit across the lot. Chase grabbed it.

"Password," his alpha said. Riel told him and swiped back the phone. He pushed the app's icon and could barely wait for the blue dot. And he waited and waited.

The screen zoomed out to display the area outside of town, then the blue dot popped on.

"What is she doing out there?" the alpha asked.

Riel was already on his way to his truck. "I'll

let you know shortly."

THIRTY-SEVEN

Sam sat in her ex-attorney's car, wondering whose side he was on. The man seemed so endearing until a few minutes ago.

She watched Carson's hand morph into a yellow-furred paw with vicious claws. Swiping at her, he said, "I suggest you sit still or my cat could become very agitated. He's not pleasant when he's upset."

Staring straight ahead, she tried to figure out what was happening. The first shock was the man she'd come to think as a grandfather was a shifter. That fact shot down a lot of options to escape.

Finally, she gave up trying to make connections. She asked, "How can you be on the dark side? At the hospital, it seemed like you really cared."

Carson tipped his head back and laughed.

"Of course, I cared. If you were dead or going to die, then I didn't have to do a thing."

"Are you behind Juan Junior and Luisa trying to kill me?"

"Of course not. Those two idiots couldn't pour piss from a boot with directions on the heel. But if they somehow succeeded, I could've sat back."

"The bomb in your office makes sense now," she said, putting it together. "You were barely there when it went off. Far enough to stay safe, but not be suspect." She couldn't believe the audacity of some people.

"Why?" Sam asked. "What did my grandmother ever do to you?" Anger grew inside her. Ginny had trusted this man with everything.

He laughed again. "It's always about the same thing — money."

With disgust, she repeated "Money?" She was about to ream him a new asshole, then images popped into her mind: his cheap suits, this old car, letting go of employees, and the sad condition of his office building.

She realized the attorney's business was about to go under. He needed money to stay open. She sighed.

"Why not just ask my grandmother for a loan or help? She believed in you her entire life."

He snorted. "She didn't believe enough. When I asked her to marry me, she turned me down, but we remained friends."

"What happened that made you do this?" Sam asked.

"Her final decision on which of her damn charities to include in the will," he answered. She recalled seeing the three names, one she didn't know. So he wanted to be included in who got the money. That was all this was.

Sam said, "There isn't anything for me to sign, is there?"

"Smart girl," he replied.

"You had this planned all along."

"Only if your aunt and cousin failed, which I figured they would with those wolf shifters always around you. Your family has no clue how much higher on the food chain we are. Stupid."

Sam wondered how her grandmother didn't see this side of Carson.

The big question floated in her mind. "You aren't listed in the will anywhere. How will killing me get you money?"

He laughed. "Sisterhoods make wonderful charities."

"Wait," Sam said, "that was the organization I didn't know in section eleven."

There was only one answer. "You changed the list Ginny gave you of organizations to give her money to, didn't you? That's the reason for all this. You were not on the list so you made up a charity no one would know or question."

Carson's face flooded red. "All the things I did for that woman, all the time I kept her from being lonely and she shows her gratitude by letting my life's work die with her. No. I won't let that happen. I will have the money."

"How did you trick her into signing your version of the will?" Sam questioned.

He frowned at her. "Really, Sam? How easily can you swap one page out for another after the signature?"

He was right. Her grandmother wouldn't have had any idea about what he did.

The buildings and sidewalks gave way to trees and ditches. She'd forgotten how nice the countryside was. For the past five years, she'd been tromping through dense jungle. She preferred this. Not that it would matter, if she were dead.

The car slowed and turned onto a rocky road, trees lining both sides.

"Where are we going?" she asked.

"A farm that belongs to a friend of a friend who's moved into assisted living and is no longer here," he answered.

So he planned to dump her body where no one would look until the place was sold. So be it, but she wasn't going to make it easy for him. She'd go down fighting for her and the baby.

With her seat belt on, there would be no jumping from the car, which wasn't high on her list, anyway.

They circled around to the back side of a falling-down barn and parked. Not far from them sat a small tractor with a front bucket like a bulldozer and a pile of dirt beside it. The mound of fresh earth lay at the end of an oval hole in the ground, just like a grave.

Holy fuck. He was going to bury her.

Panic setting in, she unbuckled her restraints and reached for the door handle. A hand of steel wrapped around her arm.

"I'm a shifter, Sam. I can hunt you down and eat you if my lion wishes. I suggest you behave."

"And just let you kill me?!" she shouted. "Are you stupid?"

His lips pressed into a thin, frowning line. As he got out of the car, he dragged her over the console between the seats and out the driver's side.

"This will be quick if you cooperate—"

"You are delusional, old man. Maybe you should give up being a lawyer." Sam didn't see his hand snap around to bash her in the face. She went down in a flurry of pain and stars in her sight.

She lay on the ground with no intention of getting up. He'd have to make her. After a swift kick to her ribs, her mind changed. If he hit her stomach, her baby could be injured.

Sam rolled onto her hands and knees, dizziness making her nauseous. Her arm was jerked up and she was back on her feet.

Every breath sent a dagger into her lungs. Her rib must've been broken. Hell, she could die before they ever got to the hole.

Sam beat on his arm, scratched at his face, thrashed to get out of his grip to no avail. Carson shoved her to the side. She felt herself falling through the air until landing hard, crumpling onto the cool dirt and blacking out.

THIRTY-EIGHT

Riel watched the street and his phone at the same time. The path of the blue dot completely puzzled him.

As far as he knew, there wasn't much more than countryside and farmland out here. It would be a good place to put something where no one would find it. Like a body.

Maybe he was overreacting. His logic was plausible, but was it probable? If not for Sam's car being taken away, he might've questioned himself. But not now.

He'd gained a lot of ground on the blue dot since leaving town. But he prayed police weren't watching for speeders right now.

His phone showed the car his mate was in turning off the road. The map didn't display a street in the car's path. He wondered where they could possibly be going.

Suddenly, the flashing point disappeared. His heart flipped, almost stopping. How would he find them now? Pressing harder on the throttle, he reached dangerous speeds on the narrow road. If anything got into his lane, it and he were mush.

He zipped by a rock road with trees lining both sides. Grass growing down its middle gave the impression of little use. Not something leading to a public place.

His hold on the phone tightened, making the plastic creak and pop. His insides wanted to explode with held in fury, anxiety, dread, and unending love for his mate. Determination drove him on, not letting fear crumple him into an inactive mess.

He'd gone a couple miles past that rock drive without seeing any other places to leave the road. Doubt set in. He should've turned back there.

Slamming on the brakes, causing the truck to fishtail, Riel made a U-turn and retraced his route to the single lane. Heading up the rocky path, he noted the silos and ramshackle barn on the hill.

The farmhouse was separated from the barn by an expanse of green grass and old, rusty tractor parts. But no vehicle. Damn it. His hand slapped the steering wheel, cracking something.

He pulled up to the barn, then reversed the truck to get back to the driveway. When he came to a stop, he heard a small engine motor like to a tractor or backhoe.

Climbing out of his vehicle, he picked up on Sam's scent. His wolf nearly came out of his skin. He raced behind the barn to see a small front-end loader pushing a pile of dirt into a hole.

He wasn't sure what was going on, but he didn't see Sam. When he got closer, he recognized Carson in the tractor's cab. And Sam's scent became stronger.

Focusing on his prey, he dove through the side of the open cab and ripped Carson from the seat and machine.

They rolled on the ground, Riel ending on top, hands around Carson's throat. "Where is Sam?"

The bastard smiled at him then shifted, tearing through his clothes. Riel knew the man was a lion from their meeting at the hospital and at the office. He should've contacted the pride's alpha, but it was too late now. If a war started between the two shifter groups, it would be his fault.

Riel saw Carson's cat glance at the backhoe and hole. The tractor was still in gear, slowly pushing the dirt into the opening. Then it clicked in his head. Sam was down there.

Before he could take a step in that direction, the lion pounced. With his own shifter's help, he dodged the claws and morphed into his own animal. It was lion versus wolf.

This fight had to be quick or Sam would be buried.

Carson paced a line keeping him from getting to his mate, daring his wolf to pass. Well, Riel wasn't playing this game. He went straight for the dirt pile.

The lion T-boned him, sending them both rolling. Clawing, biting, and shoving, Riel fought for the life of the only love he'd ever have. She was everything to him. Without her, life wasn't worth his time. He would do whatever it took to save her.

He broke away from the cat and dug his claws into the ground, tearing his way toward the hole. In order to stop the tractor, he'd have to shift into his human form. That would leave him vulnerable to the lion.

Then he heard Sam's scream coming from the pit. Adrenaline poured through him, giving him extra strength and speed. But how was he going to save her without dying first?

He let out a howl, hoping she would

understand he was there. She yelled his name and he felt reassured she knew he wouldn't give up on her.

Running toward the front-end loader, he had an idea. His wolf was on board, but not happy about the acrobatics involved.

He slowed to make sure the cat was close and received a clawed swat on his ass. Picking up a bit of speed, he prepared for the maneuver. The tractor was only a few feet ahead. At the last second, he dropped to the ground and slid under the machine's frame.

As he hoped, the bigger lion wasn't prepared for such a move and slammed into the engine housing, tipping the tractor onto two wheels, then completely onto its side.

While the cat was rebounding, Riel dashed to Sam, shifting when reaching the opening.

"Sam!" he hollered, sliding to his knees. The hole was at least seven feet deep and half filled with dirt. Sam was digging herself out, which lifted some of the panic from his mind. She was alive and would stay that way.

"Carson is trying to kill me!" she shouted to him. He saw the cat stand and shake its head.

"I gathered that," he replied.

"Smart ass," she said. "What's the plan?"

"I'll distract the lion while you get your cute ass inside my truck." He stood and strode away from his mate. "Hey, pussy," Riel waved his arms to get the beast's attention on him, "think you can take on a real man, flesh and blood?"

The animal swung its head around to face him, a low growl coming through clenched jaws.

"That's it, old man. This way. Any shifter can beat up on a human, but to get to my mate, you'll have to go through me."

The cat stopped, shifted, then Carson climbed to his two feet. "Your mate?" He stepped toward Riel. "That's why Ginny kept you around. I knew you weren't fucking her but couldn't figure out why she'd want a stinking dog nearby."

"For a shifter," Riel started, still backing away, "you're pretty damn senseless. Couldn't you smell and see she didn't want you around? She pegged your true self, a selfish bastard willing to kill for some money."

Carson frowned. "Not some money, dog. Billions."

He whistled while in his periphery vision he saw Sam crawl out of the earthen prison. "Not a bad payday if you'd made it work. But you didn't. Time to tuck your tail between your legs and run home, old man."

Carson growled, "I'll show you old man." He dove forward, shifting on the fly. Riel took off running toward the house. When reaching the junk pile with rusted farm equipment, he glanced back to see where Sam was. That's when his foot caught on a metal pipe, tripping him.

He rolled onto his back as the lion sprang for the kill.

THIRTY-NINE

Sam clawed her way up the side of the hole and climbed out. Looking around, she saw Riel and Carson, but no truck.

She did know where the car was, though. With her head pounding and slightly sore ribs, she rushed to the jalopy. As she remembered, the keys were in the ignition.

She cranked the engine and spun the car around, heading for the house. Coming around the side of the barn, her heart stopped seeing the lion standing over Ry's human form. But her mate held a beam under the cat's throat, lifting it back, keeping it from raking his face off.

Staring at the animal's ass end, Sam gunned the engine, jerking the vehicle forward. "You bastard," she yelled, "get off my mate!" The front of the car slammed into the lion's hindquarters, sending him ass over heels.

She jumped out of the car and ran to Ry. "Are you hurt?" she asked, roaming her eyes over his very naked body.

He shook his head and sat up. "I'll be fine." The cat roared. Dammit, why wasn't it dead? Not that she tried to kill it, just free her man.

An unfamiliar voice hollered from the driveway. "Stand down, Carson." The cat slunk back a step and growled at the newcomers. Chase stepped out of his truck while a man she didn't know climbed from the passenger's side.

Riel got to his feet. "That's the lion pride alpha. Count on one alpha calling the other in an emergency."

Carson shifted to human and inched his way closer. Sam figured with his boss here, the attorney would leave without issue. But money made people do stupid-ass things.

Talons extended from shifted hands, Carson lunged at them standing together. As the team Sam and Ry were, they shoved him away.

The old man stumbled backward into the junk pit, impaling himself on a metal fence post, painted white and green steel protruding from his chest.

EPILOGUE

"Tryx," a very pregnant Sam said as she and the women were gathered at a table in Tryx's pastry shop, "your baking ovens are straight from heaven." Sam licked frosting from her fingers.

Tryx laughed. "Is the right response thank you? Didn't know I had divine appliances."

Sophia snorted. "Your entire display cabinet is from the Almighty."

"Okay," Tryx said, "I have magic mixing bowls." She gestured that she was ready to get back to the original conversation. "Now tell me again what the attorney said. He was in love with your grandmother?"

Sam shrugged. "He said that, but I don't know."

Nat said, "You'd think if he really loved her, then he wouldn't want to see her granddaughter dead, much less be the one to kill her."

Tryx shifted in her chair. "And your aunt and cousin weren't in cahoots with him?"

"No," Sam replied, "that's why no one ever suspected him. He knew at least one person in my family would try to off me—"

"But Riel saved you every time," Juliet gushed. Tryx sighed while everyone else looked at her. All of them but her had a guy. And it seemed Nat had two. Life just wasn't fair in the love department.

Juliet laid a hand on Tryx's. "You'll find the right guy when the time is right."

"Yeah," Tryx said, "will I still be alive?"

"You've got a point," Nat said. "Maybe he's the one in heaven sending you the oven and mixing bowls."

Tryx snorted. "Well, he definitely isn't alive within twenty miles of here. Between coffee and cake, I've seen every person in this town and there's been no butt sniffing." She laughed among their groans.

"That's it," Sophia said, clapping her hands together.

"What?" Tryx asked.

"You need a vacation," Sophia continued. "When was the last time you were away?"

"You mean before the last time I stayed in bed after five a.m.? Before I went home every night with flour in places beach sand doesn't even go?"

"Ew," Nat whispered. "Remind me to never open a bakery."

"No worries, Nat," Sam said. "Troy will take care of any stray flour."

"Troy?" Nat questioned. The other shifters, ducking out of Nat's view at the table, made frantic motions for Sam to zip her lips.

Tryx could only laugh. Kane and Troy were a riot, but someone was going to get their ass kicked, and not in a good way.

"Anyway," Sophia pushed, "do you have any family out of town you can visit?" Tryx shook her head. Everyone in her family had stayed close over the years.

"What about friends?" Juliet asked. "From college or something?"

An adorable freckled face of a boy popped into her mind. The guy was her best friend for one summer camp. When she was, like, ten.

Tryx was being picked on for being a shifter and the boy stood up for her, telling the others to go away before he shifted into his animal and ate them. Needless to say, that didn't go over well with the counselors. But Tryx would never forget him or what he did for her.

"Maybe," Tryx said. "You girls would have to take over the bakery or you might have a mutiny from the coffee addicted citizens."

"Deal," they all said together.

Oh shit, Tryx gulped. What had she just gotten herself into?

The End

ABOUT THE AUTHOR

New York Times and USA Today Bestselling Author

Hi! I'm Milly Taiden. I love to write sexy stories featuring fun, sassy heroines with curves and growly alpha males with fur. My books are a great way to satisfy your craving for paranormal romance with action, humor, suspense and happily ever afters.

I live in Florida with my hubby, our kids, and our fur babies: Speedy, Stormy and Teddy. I have a serious addiction to chocolate and cake.

I love to meet new readers, so come sign up for my newsletter and check out my Facebook page. We always have lots of fun stuff going on there.

SIGN UP FOR MILLY'S NEWSLETTER FOR

LATEST NEWS!

http://eepurl.com/pt9q1

Find out more about Milly here:

www.millytaiden.com

Find out more about Milly Taiden here:

Email: milly@millytaiden.com

Website: http://www.millytaiden.com

Facebook: http://www.facebook.com/millytaidenpage

Twitter: https://www.twitter.com/millytaiden

If you liked this story, you might also enjoy the following by Milly Taiden:

Sassy Mates / Sassy Ever After Series

Scent of a Mate *Book One*

A Mate's Bite *Book Two*

Unexpectedly Mated *Book Three*

A Sassy Wedding *Short 3.7*

The Mate Challenge *Book Four*

Sassy in Diapers *Short 4.3*

Fighting for Her Mate *Book Five*

A Fang in the Sass *Book 6*

Also, check out the **Sassy Ever After World on Amazon**

Or visit http://mtworldspress.com

Nightflame Dragons

Dragons' Jewel *Book One*

Dragons' Savior *Book Two*

Dragons' Bounty *Book Three (coming soon)*

A.L.F.A Series

Elemental Mating *Book One*

Mating Needs *Book Two*

Dangerous Mating *Book Three*

Fearless Mating *Book Four*

Savage Shifters

Savage Bite *Book One*

Savage Kiss *Book Two*

Savage Hunger *Book Three*

Drachen Mates

Bound in Flames *Book One*

Bound in Darkness *Book Two*

Bound in Eternity *Book Three*

Bound in Ashes *Book Four*

Federal Paranormal Unit

Wolf Protector *Federal Paranormal Unit Book One*

Dangerous Protector *Federal Paranormal Unit Book Two*

Unwanted Protector *Federal Paranormal Unit Book Three*

Deadly Protector *Federal Paranormal Unit Book Four*

(Coming Soon)

Paranormal Dating Agency

Twice the Growl *Book One*

Geek Bearing Gifts *Book Two*

The Purrfect Match *Book Three*

Curves 'Em Right *Book Four*

Tall, Dark and Panther *Book Five*

The Alion King *Book Six*

There's Snow Escape *Book Seven*

Scaling Her Dragon *Book Eight*

In the Roar *Book Nine*

Scrooge Me Hard *Short One*

Bearfoot and Pregnant *Book Ten*

All Kitten Aside *Book Eleven*

Oh My Roared *Book Twelve*

Piece of Tail *Book Thirteen*

Kiss My Asteroid *Book Fourteen*

Scrooge Me Again *Short Two*

Born with a Silver Moon *Book Fifteen*

Sun in the Oven *Book Sixteen*

Between Ice and Frost *Book Seventeen*

Scrooge Me Again *Book Eighteen*

Winter Takes All *Book Nineteen*

You're Lion to Me *Book Twenty*

Also, check out the **Paranormal Dating Agency World**

on Amazon

Or visit http://mtworldspress.com

Raging Falls

Miss Taken *Book One*

Miss Matched *Book Two*

Miss Behaved *Book Three*

Miss Behaved *Book Three*

Miss Mated *Book Four*

Miss Conceived *Book Five (Coming Soon)*

FUR-ocious Lust - Bears

Fur-Bidden *Book One*

Fur-Gotten *Book Two*

Fur-Given Book *Three*

FUR-ocious Lust - Tigers

Stripe-Tease *Book Four*

Stripe-Search *Book Five*

Stripe-Club *Book Six*

Night and Day Ink

Bitten by Night *Book One*

Seduced by Days *Book Two*

Mated by Night *Book Three*

Taken by Night *Book Four*

Dragon Baby *Book Five*

Shifters Undercover

Bearly in Control *Book One*

Fur Fox's Sake *Book Two*

Black Meadow Pack

Sharp Change *Black Meadows Pack Book One*

Caged Heat *Black Meadows Pack Book Two*

Other Works

Wolf Fever

Fate's Wish

Wynter's Captive

Sinfully Naughty Vol. 1

Don't Drink and Hex

Hex Gone Wild

Hex and Kisses

Alpha Owned

Match Made in Hell

Alpha Geek

HOWLS Romances

The Wolf's Royal Baby

The Wolf's Bandit

Goldie and the Bears

Her Fairytale Wolf *Co-Written*

The Wolf's Dream Mate *Co-Written*

Her Winter Wolves *Co-Written*

The Alpha's Chase *Co-Written*

Contemporary Works

Mr. Buff

Stranded Temptation

Lucky Chase

Their Second Chance

Club Duo Boxed Set

A Hero's Pride

A Hero Scarred

A Hero for Sale

Wounded Soldiers Set

If you enjoyed the book, please consider leaving a review, even if it's only a line or two; it would make all the difference and would be very much appreciated.

Thank you!

Made in the USA
Coppell, TX
20 February 2020

16027717R00157